Fox Hollow

VERDA SPICE

DEDICATION

To my sister, the author, and all who, just like her,
believe doing a good piece of work has its own rewards...

To the reader:

Manuscript lost? Is anything lost if no one is looking for it?

In March of 2020, our world plunged into one of separation and isolation thanks to the Covid 19 pandemic. Being empty-nesters, my wife and I soon bored of binge watching TV and just looking at each other. Probably like many others, to end the boredom, we started a massive deep-cleaning project that began in our basement and went up through our two living levels and into our attic. We sorted everything into keep, sell, giveaway, or toss. A particularly worn old box with several movers labels on it emerged and was opened; its contents to be distributed to the various piles. From this box came an old large manila envelope addressed to me when we lived in California. It was from my sister in Indiana. The post mark on the envelope was December, 1986. Thanks to my natural gift of pack-rattery, this envelope had survived 35 years and moves from California to Pennsylvania to Ohio to West Virginia and, now, back to Pennsylvania. I opened the envelope and a draft of Fox Hollow slid into my hands. I remembered the author, my sister, sending it to me to read. I recalled how much I enjoyed the book, not only on its own merits, but because it has a special meaning for me due to the setting. As a very young boy, we lived in that part of rural Indiana. Right across the gravel road from our house was a long, densely forested valley known as Fox Hollow. We moved into town in 1952 and this story is set in the mid 1960's, but the rough countryside, twisty up and down narrow roads, the country store, the little church with its parsonage, open pastures and deep, dark woods all came to life for me through my sister's writing.

So. Which pile to put this in, sell, give, throw, or set back in a box somewhere? Thirty-five years and I hadn't done anything with it. That got me thinking... thirty-five years and my sister hadn't done anything with it! Maybe it isn't as good as I remembered. To be sure, I read it again.

OK! That wasn't it, it is as good as I remembered. It is as good or better than any of the romance/drama movies I "accidently" listen to or watch on TV. That prompted a call to the author. When I asked her, her answer kind of boiled down to her task was to write the story and she did that. She was content with that. She told me she had no plans for Fox Hollow. When I asked her if she would mind if I made plans for Fox Hollow, she gave me free rein with it. (She also told me I could dedicate it to whoever I wanted to. I wanted to dedicate it to her but I knew that would not please her.... so I have dedicated it to her - a person content with doing a good job - without calling her by name... don't tell her, OK?)

Fox Hollow. Even if you are not from or familiar with the hills and hollars of Eastern Greene County, Indiana, I hope that you enjoy reading Verda's book as much as I have. After you finish reading it, go find a stable that has trails to ride. If you can, stop and look across the pasture and to the woods line. Just sit in the saddle and think back, and imagine... you are in Fox Hollow.

Warmest Regards,

Mike Baines

Fox Hollow

One

The road narrowed coming into the hairpin curves forcing me to slow my car and hug the centerline. I had forgotten how dangerously close to the ravines were the uphill twists and turns of the county road, blacktopped now, not graveled as I remembered.

But I found holding to a more sensible speed did nothing to stop the sensation that I was racing headlong toward a disaster of my own making. When I left this part of Southern Indiana, I was an unhappy, frightened girl of fourteen. Today, ending an absence of several years, I was almost too nervous to keep my mind on my driving. Even now I could not ignore the uneasiness that had traveled with me all the way from Wilmington, North Carolina.

Again, I tried to block those recurring thoughts with the soft, late April beauty of the countryside around me. My spirits lifted. Fox Hollow was just ahead---just around the next bend!

The years I had spent away with Aunt Megan had not lessened my love for this place---nor had they eased the hurt of being ordered from it by my father.

My father and I had shared a stormy relationship at best, as I could never accept the fact that we Jordane's made our living from the deaths of wild animals. For Fox Hollow is a modestly famous retreat offering the affluent an assortment of organized hunts. The most popular of these, and the most controversial, has always been the fox hunt.

Now and then feeble complaints were made about the horrible way the fox was killed---torn apart by the hounds---but Fox Hollow was a much needed source of extra income to most people in the area, so no one protested too loudly. No one wanted to risk losing favor with Thomas Jordane.

But father had been forced to make one large concession to the changing times. It was the custom when a fox hunt ended in a kill to mark the foreheads of first-time riders with the blood of the fox. One such hunt had been made up largely of students from Indiana University. They had gone back to campus proudly flaunting their "mark of courage", creating such a stir that articles were printed in the campus paper denouncing the violence done in the guise of sport. The cry was taken up in other local publications and father agreed to stop the killing to squelch the damaging publicity.

Since that time, the fox was hunted until cornered, then the hounds were called off. This had not had the adverse effect father had expected and Fox Hollow continued to flourish.

In father's private life, the one person whose opinion mattered to him was Aunt Megan, widow of father's younger brother. Even my mother's thoughts, when she had dared to voice them, were ignored if they were contrary to father's. But to Megan, he tried endlessly to defend the livelihood he knew she detested. Young as I was at that time, I had known he longed for her approval, as I had longed in vain for his. And I knew that like me, he fell short, in spite of his heated self-defense...

"I know what's said about me, but every young buck in Greene County will be pawing at the ground by the time Ellen is of age; they all know she'll be worth plenty one of these days. These same country-bumpkins that are so quick to take my money for their beef and vegetables resent me for capitalizing on what they did only for their own sport--- they'd all give their eldest son for a set-up like Fox Hollow!"

And that, I had soon learned, was just what father was counting on. The eldest son or the youngest, it wouldn't matter. I was to marry and provide Fox Hollow with the one thing it lacked---a male heir.

I had never forgotten a snatch of conversation I'd overheard between father and Aunt Megan the day after my mother's funeral.

It could still bring that unhappy time back to think of it... "I've lost my son and now my wife! Ellen is all I have to keep Fox Hollow going! I'm counting on her to marry someone who'll take an interest in this place---she owes me that!"

"Thomas, Claudette's death has been difficult for Ellen, let me take her back to North Carolina for a visit"

"Ellen has never had anything difficult. Claudette

used no discipline with her, but now I'm going to see that she learns to run this household!"

"That shouldn't stop her from visiting---surely you can give us that time together!"

My aunt had sounded close to tears and I'd ran outside to keep from hearing more fearing I would learn I was somehow the cause of her tears.

Now I gave my attention completely to the present as I neared the small, brick church and two-story, white frame house on my right. My mother and I had once attended this church faithfully. But at the death of my little brother, father had forbidden it, saying it obviously had been a waste of our time and his money. He had insulted Reverend Flagg further by having a minister from one of the in-town churches officiate at the funeral.

I stopped the car and stared. How could it all look so unchanged---and Rachel Flagg---would she seem a stranger to me now? We had been best friends, Rachel and I, her brother, John, and his friend, Rex Post---where were they now---

A curtain was pulled back from a window and I saw Rachel's father peering out. The Reverend Flagg, like most people, had never been inclined to think very well of the Jordane's. I did not yet feel up to discovering if that had changed. I drove on, a bit embarrassed at having given in to my impulse to stop.

Turning off the county road, I drove through the fieldstone columns that marked, rather defiantly I'd always thought, the entrance to Fox Hollow. Here my father had succeeded in creating a world of his own---and how he loved his role as its ruler!

When father bought this land from Bertha and Ersey Hunter who stayed on to work for him, it had seldom been seen by anyone not born in Greene County. At that time the surrounding area had doled out a sparse living to a few farmers, a country store and one small church. But for the most part the land had been inhabited by wild game. Rabbits and squirrels were hunted for food, raccoon and fox for sport, especially fox, for both the red and grey were plentiful.

Seeing it now, it was hard to believe I had ever lived here, that I had roamed the woods as freely as the foxes that gave this valley its name.

I stopped the car near a cedar grove and got out. The pink and white of blooming redbud and dogwood trees mingled with the cedar's vivid green. Walking under the fragrant branches, I felt a surge of affection for the stately trees. Once I had played here for hours at a time. The trees had seemed huge to me and I'd felt safe among them. They had talked to me when the wind blew through them, making my name sound like the loveliest name in the world.

I waited---but it was as if the old cedars had forgotten me, or perhaps, like myself, they were only surprised at my presence.

"Please remember me---I'm Ellen!" I fought back a foolish urge to cry and turned toward the car.

Just ahead of me a dog dashed across the drive, intent on following a scent. I stared after it. It had looked so much like Braidy, the dog I'd owned as a child. I got in the car and sat a moment. Poor old Braidy. He had earned his name by patiently wearing the chains of daisies I braided and placed about his neck. He came to Fox Hollow as a homeless stray; to my surprise and delight, I was allowed to keep him. But he became an innocent victim in one of father's lessons on the importance of being a thoroughbred. I could never forget what father said and did that day---

"Ellen, I'm going to teach you I mean what I say! At Fox Hollow I do not keep anything that isn't pureblooded---if it isn't an asset, I get rid of it!"

I had stared at the gunnysack he held, hearing the tiny whimpers.

"My best bitch just whelped this litter, sired by that mongrel of yours. I told you to keep that mutt away from the kennels!"

I had known what he was going to do, but my begging was useless. When we reached the creek, he swung the sack in the air and let it go. It arched high above the water before it hit and quickly sank.

Father marched me up to the stables. He went in and came back out with a rifle. Braidy was trotting around us and I'd grabbed his collar.

"Ellen, let that mutt loose!"

"No!" I had started to cry, unable to help the tears that I know would only make father angrier. But Braidy tired of my hard grip and twisted free, loping off toward the kennels. I'd called frantically, but Braidy just stood looking at me and wagging his tail.

Taking quick aim, father shot, then walked away without a word. I had seen the sympathy in the faces of the men tending the horses when I had gone into the stables for a shovel. I just shook my head at their offers to bury Braidy. But Ersey Hunter said it was "no fit job for a girl" and together we wrapped Braidy in a scarlet hunting jacket father had neglected to take to the house, then we buried my pet.

And I had planned to get even---with the help of Rachel and John Flagg and Rex Post I'd sabotage the first fox hunt of the new season.

Our plans were made, there would be smoke screens to get the young dogs off the scent and bogus bugle blowing to confuse the new riders. John and Rex would put down a false trail to put off the seasoned hounds---all harmless things.

But my mother had decided to ride in the hunt, she was thrown off her horse and two days later she died from her injuries. I didn't yet know how father found out I had had a part in the sabotage attempt, amateurish as it was. But he knew, and in a black rage he sent me away from Fox Hollow---as he had said, if something was not an asset, he got rid of it---

I rolled up the car window. The breeze was cooler now that the sun was slipping behind the range of hills to the west. I shivered with the same dread I had felt as a child when I had stayed out in the woods too long and knew I would be punished by Bertha, our housekeeper, or worst of all, my father. Thomas Jordane's temper flared hot and fast and was slow to cool, a fact I knew well! If my mother had a temper it was never directed at me, nor were any other emotions she might have felt. I had grown up knowing there was no love between my parents. Rachel Flagg had told me the whole county knew my father had married Claudette Myers just for the inheritance she would receive. I had seen nothing between my parents to contradict Rachel's gossip.

Jerking the car into motion, I drove on to the point where the drive overlooked the valley. I braked, giving myself time to take in the open meadows neatly trimmed with a ricrac of wooden fence running away from the slate-roofed buildings into the deep woods.

And there was the house. Still with its air of being impervious to the turmoil created by its inhabitants, as imposing in its size as I'd always found it. It was a house that stirred my emotions even during the years I was away if I but thought of it---the house I had grown up in and had so wanted to belong in.

When I reached the front door I hesitated, then lifted the brass fox-head knocker. When it opened, Bertha Hunter stood gaping at me. She had been the housekeeper at Fox Hollow since I could remember. I had always known she didn't like me and now her expression made it clear nothing had changed. She stood blocking the door offering no invitation to enter.

I brushed past and walked from the hall into the 'front' room, as the largest and most formal room in the house was called. For so long I had wondered how it would feel to be in this old house again! It seemed just as large to me now as when I was a child.

Behind me, Bertha's tone was scathing. "Well, well! If the prodigal daughter ain't come back!"

She was wasting no time in reminding me I was still unwelcome in my father's house. At one time she would have made me quake inwardly, now I was pleased to find myself undaunted.

"That word hardly applies, Bertha, prodigal means extravagant, and I was never that!" I could see it still angered her to be corrected, especially by me. "But it does look as if father has loosened the purse strings."

The house was filled with pieces that looked new and

expensive, mixing nicely with things that were obviously quite old. One such table with a marble top I could remember very well, as I'd often spent my time polishing its ornate legs.

"Just too bad if you don't like it. It really ain't none of your business!"

"But I do like it. Very much." My unexpected approval surprised her, and I enjoyed setting Bertha back on her heels.

"Well, we got the big party in a few days, seemed like a good time to spruce things up. This was a real good season, and your father is gonna throw some humdinger of a---it's gonna be a real elegant affair!"

Bertha was returning my stare and it seemed to me she was determined not to be the first to look away. "I'd like to see my father, Bertha, where is he?"

"In his study. I'll announce you."

Announce me? I was sure Bertha was trying to impress me. My mother had tried for years to improve Bertha's speech, but father had only laughed and said that the city slickers liked to hear Bertha talk, she lent some flavor to Fox Hollow.

"You needn't bother, Bertha, don't let me keep you from anything." But Bertha followed along as I tapped on the study door, a bit more timidly than I'd intended.

"Well! Hello, Ellen." There was no more warmth in his voice than if I'd been a stranger selling cosmetics door to door.

"Hello, Father." I could find nothing more to say. My mind seemed blocked by his icy reserve. He was as unapproachable as ever.

"Where is Megan---she is with you?"

The eagerness he let slip into his voice prodded an all but forgotten memory---once I had seen him kiss Megan lightly as she was leaving Fox Hollow after one of her rare visits. It was an act so out of character for my father that I had never understood it. But I knew he would be much happier to see my aunt than he was at seeing me.

"I came alone. I'll be managing Megan's shop."

He motioned me toward a chair and closed the study door, leaving Betha still standing in the hall where I was certain she would waste no time in getting her ear to the door.

Father leaned back in his chair. "So, you are going to run the shop---Megan considers you capable?"

Now his face held only a pretense of interest. He had always acted as if Megan's shops were merely a hobby, and a poor choice of one at that. I had never understood his attitude and now it stirred my anger.

"I'm quite capable! I've studied marketing and I have first-hand experience from the shop in Wilmington---Megan took me on buying trips---I know what I'm doing!"

"We'll certainly see. I assume you are still unmarried?"

He had not changed---where I was concerned that was all that held his interest. Whatever else I might accomplish, it would never gain me his approval. He had not even hinted he was sorry for the years of silence between us.

"I'm not interested in marriage. I enjoy my work and I'll be giving it all my time!" I snapped the words.

"Now hold on, Ellen, no reason to be so touchy."

"I'm not! At least, I wasn't---we haven't seen each other in nearly eight years! I expected---I don't know just what I expected, but I should have known better!"

"I expected certain things from you in the past, Ellen, and I was bitterly disappointed, yet you expect me to forget all that when you walk in the door?"

He was looking at me with his face as dark and blaming as the day he sent me away.

"Alright, Father, say what's on your mind. It's a few years overdue, but let's get it out in the open." I could see my calm approach surprised him, but he covered it quickly.

"You're right, it is overdue---I sent you away because I could not accept that my own daughter would plot to tear down what I'd worked so hard and long to build! Bertha told me you and your friends planned a sabotage---due to Claudette's accident a sabotage was unnecessary. The hunt was ruined at the start. Still, I could not allow you to remain."

"I know---you once told me that you would get rid of whatever was not an asset to Fox Hollow! Are you trying to tell me you blame me for what happened?"

"No. As usual Claudette had been drinking that morning. Otherwise she would not have dared to oppose me and ride in the hunt. Ersey told me her horse was skittish--- it had not been ridden in some time and the excitement of the hunt made it unpredictable It shied away from a jump at the last moment and Claudette lost her balance---"

I let out a deep breath. Ersey was Bertha's husband and father's righthand man. Ersey was the only person at Fox Hollow who had shown me any genuine affection. In his awkward, shy way he had been my only friend here.

"---otherwise, "my father continued, "I would have thought your irresponsible nature was once again the cause of a tragedy. But the point is, in view of the reason I sent you away I fail to see how you can expect a hero's welcome now that you've decided, unwisely I suspect, to return!"

I stared at the man now standing across the room. His tall, broad shouldered frame filled his brown tweed jacket as solidly as ever, his dark auburn hair showed no grey and his face held a healthy tan. His grey-green eyes were bright on me.

"What are you talking about---another tragedy---"

"There is no use in going back over all that---I'm only interested in what you do from here on. I can see Megan did you some good, you seem to know how to dress and wear your hair---you'll turn a few heads! I'll wager you won't be so disinterested in marriage for long. There'll be young bucks from all around wanting to be first in line! And the day you take one on you can live here again---you and your husband! Fox Hollow will be your home!"

He was really smiling for the first time, looking as if he had offered me the moon. It was the same old story---I was to marry and as soon as possible present him with a grandson. As merely his daughter, I did not qualify for the honor of inheriting Fox Hollow.

The last small hope that I could untangle the threads

of our meager relationship vanished and I wanted only to be away from him.

"It was a long trip and I'm tired. Bertha told me you had a good season. I'm sure you're busy planning your celebration. I just came to tell you I was back. I can't think now why I thought it would matter." I crossed the room and my hand was on the doorknob when he spoke.

"Ellen---didn't Megan even send a message?"

I shook my head. I could tell it was a question he had tried not to ask. For just an instant I could see his deep disappointment before he changed the subject.

"The annual bash for the local yokels is this Saturday. Why don't you come---there will be people here you know and some you should meet? After all, a good businesswoman wouldn't pass up an opportunity to spread some good will. Surely some of these hicks can afford to patronize your shop!"

I had forgotten just how arrogant he could be. "I'll think about the party." I tossed my answer over my shoulder as I left.

I hurried out of the house to my car. I felt none too steady and I waited a moment until I was calmer. So--- nothing had changed. I had to admit that now. I would stop thinking about my father and concentrate on the shop.

As I drove back to town I knew I had not found what I'd hoped for---what I could not even name, for it was as elusive as the mist now filling the valleys.

In my motel room I made a quick call to Megan to let her know I had arrived safely, then prepared for bed hoping sleep would come quickly. But I kept hearing Megan's voice---her concern for me had been so obvious, as had been her relief that I was not staying at Fox Hollow. I was sure it had not entered father's mind to invite me, he would not think I was entitled.

Had I imagined Megan's concern, or simply misunderstood---no doubt such was the case. I shrugged it off as the result of being so bone-tired. It had been an unnerving day and I was becoming melodramatic.

Plumping up the pillows, I settled into their softness,

but it was no use. Megan's concern, real or imagined, had rekindled my own uneasiness.

There had been something at Fox Hollow those last few years I lived there that I had been glad to escape. It was strong, yet intangible when I tried to pin it down. Megan felt it, I could always tell from her voice each time we spoke of Fox Hollow.

My homecoming had been nothing like the daydreams I'd spent so much time fabricating over the years, with even Bertha glad to see me! I pictured her as she'd looked when she opened the door to me---blocking my way with her arms crossed over her large body and her small, black eyes stinging at me like two angry sweat-bees.

And my father---unforgiving and unyielding. Megan had warned me not to expect anything else. "Even trees know to bend with the wind to keep from splintering," she had said, but not Thomas Jordane.

And finally, I allowed myself to think of Mitch Kramer, the one reason I'd been eager to return that no one, not even Megan, knew about. What would his face tell me when we met?

The telephone rang, surprising me out of my thoughts. It could only be Megan---no one at Fox Hollow had been told where to reach me---"Hello."

"Better run back to Megan, Foxey-Locksey, no one wants you here, better run while you can!"

"Who is this?" But the line was dead before my question was out and I slowly hung up.

The words had been so muffled I could not tell if it had been a man or a woman speaking. Was it Bertha---she knew Megan stayed here at the Hearthside Inn when she came on shop business and would assume I would stay here also. I was sure Bertha was the one behind the call and I'd settle things with her soon enough! Anger stiffened my determination---I was back and I was staying! Megan needed me here and I would never let her down.

I went back to bed and tried to relax. I was anxious for morning, and at last, sometime during my uneasy sleep, it arrived.

Two

To avoid the possibility of another mysterious call, I checked out of the Hearthside Inn. Later, I would find another motel. I drove to a nearby restaurant for breakfast. It was a perfect spring morning and my elation at being back returned.

I found myself watching for familiar faces as people came and went. I knew I was really looking for Mitch, though I didn't know for certain he was still here---but just the thought that he could be was making my heart beat faster!

Was it really possible to love someone you hadn't seen in so long? But I knew the answer, for me at least. Mitch had left an impression on my life that no amount of time could change. He had treated me as no one, except Megan, ever had---always kind and thoughtful, never teasing, he talked with me and listened to me---and always I'd seen something in his eyes that reached out to me.

I drove on to the downtown area and parked near the shop. Megan bought it three years ago but I had never seen it. She had never told me exactly why she wanted the shop, but now I was sure she had seen it as a way to give me the choice of returning if I wished. As always, Megan was trying to smooth the way for me.

THE VOGUE---the letters were drab and faded, blending into the grey of the building until they were hardly noticeable. There was an awning across the front, making the window dark in spite of its lighting. There was one mannequin dressed in a black and white suit I recognized as a Lily Ann. It was lovely, but I was sure it would catch no one's eye in such a bland setting.

I pushed the door open and was announced by the tin clang of a bell. A small, brown suited lady came tiredly toward me.

"May I help you?"

"Are you Mrs. Birkdale? I'm Ellen Jordane."

"Oh, Miss Jordane! I'm so glad to meet you, so glad you're here! I'm at the end of my wits trying to get everything in order for Mrs. Jordane, well, your mother I mean, but thank goodness you're here now! I had expected Mrs. Jordane to come herself, but I guess you'll know what to do. My husband has just retired, and we plan to travel just as soon as I can get away---"

"Please, Mrs. Birkdale!" Her chirping little voice left me breathless, as she talked her thin hands fluttered in the air and I had to stifle the impulse to hold them still. I felt I already had the reasons for the decline in sales the shop was suffering. "Now, first of all, Megan Jordane is my aunt, not my mother---"

"Oh, yes, I'm sure I knew that at one time, but I'd forgotten. I so seldom see Mrs. Jordane and I'd never met you, so with your names being the same I just---"

"It's alright, Mrs. Birkdale. I need to know if you have placed any ads in the newspaper this week. Are you running any special promotion at this time?"

"Oh, mercy no! I've got too much to do as it is! Trudy comes in on Fridays and Saturdays to help, otherwise it's all up to me."

"Good. I'm going to close the shop for a short time."

"Whatever for?" She was regarding me as if she doubted my sanity.

"To redecorate, check the lines we carry and acquaint myself with the shop books. You needn't stay. If I need something, I'll call. I'm closing the shop today."

"My, my! Just like that! Well, whatever you say, Miss Jordane! Things sure happen fast sometimes don't they? But my husband will be happy, he's impatient to get going and so am I---"

"Mrs. Birkdale!" She blinked and stopped talking. "Megan is confident you've done your best for her. She asked me to give you this and to relay her best wishes to you and Mr. Birkdale. I expect she will call you this evening."

"Oh, thank you! She took the envelope and to my surprise opened it immediately. "How generous of your aunt! Yes indeed, very generous---"

"I'm sure you have a lot to do, Mrs. Birkdale, so why don't you go along. I'll manage just fine."

She nodded and shuffled to the back of the shop. She returned with her purse and a light coat.

"Here are my keys, dearie, and you just call if you need me!"

The only thing about Mrs. Birkdale that moved without effort seemed to be her tongue. When at last she was out the door, I locked it and pulled the shade.

Megan had said she was giving me a free hand, and I was sure she would have approved of my decision. It had been hastily made, but there was no other choice. The interior of the shop was as drab as the outside.

I placed a notice in the Bloomington TRIBUNE to explain the temporary closing and made appointments with three interior decorators before I let myself stop to think about anything else. Then I turned through the directory to find some familiar names---R. Flagg---it had to be Rachel---I turned to the K's. Yes---Mitch was listed---but he won't be home this late in the morning---is he married? ---I gave in and dialed his number. There was no answer and I hung up feeling foolish---that proves nothing, you know, I chided myself.

I turned back to Rachel's number and dialed. It rang several times while I wondered what she was doing now---perhaps she was a teacher or maybe a nurse, probably she wasn't even home---

"Hello---" the voice was sleepy and impatient.

"Rachel? Rachel Flagg?"

"Yes, who is this and what do you want?"

"It's Ellen Jordane."

There was silence, then an excited voice. "Ellen, is it really you---where are you?"

"I'm here in town, at the shop. I want to see you, may I come over?"

"Ellen, let me come there. What shop are you talking about?"

"Megan's shop---The Vogue. It's closed, so just knock on the door---I can't wait to see you!"

"I'll be right there---I'll hurry!"

While I waited, I looked the shop over. The shelves were dusty and the date on the register was three days behind. I thumbed thru the order books. There would be no large deliveries of new stock for a time. That had worked out in my favor as I would not be here to sign for anything on a regular basis until the shop was open again.

There was a knock at the door. I hurried to open it and Rachel and I stood staring at each other.

"Rachel! It's so good to see you---I really have missed you!"

She hugged me. "Ellen! Why didn't you write?"

"After all the trouble we were in over that silly sabotage attempt I knew your father wouldn't let you write to me so I sent a few letters to you in care of my father, thinking Bertha would get them to you."

"Bertha didn't deliver them, and she wouldn't even give me your address. She said you'd left Fox Hollow for good and didn't want any reminders! I finally believed her."

"Well, I'm here now, to stay! I guess you didn't know Aunt Meg owns this shop. Business has been so bad that she took Mrs. Birkdale's retirement as a chance to straighten things out---that's my job---I'm the manager---can you imagine that?"

"For whatever reason, I'm glad you're back---does John know?"

"No one knows but you, and father and Bertha, I just arrived yesterday. Now, tell me what you're doing."

She looked at me steadily. "Ellen, remember one day when we talked about changing our lives so we could be happy? Well, I'm still trying to do that!"

I laughed. "So am I!" I led her to two small chairs near the dressing rooms. "Listen, this Saturday night is the postseason party my father throws each spring---come with me! He invited me, to my surprise. It'd be fun if you come too."

"It might be, at that! But you have to know something first, Ellen, everyone else around fox Hollow does---my father, the esteemed Reverend Flagg, has stepped down as pastor of his little flock because of me, because he considers me a fallen woman and a blot on his otherwise spotless reputation! So, if the folks from the old neighborhood see you with me, well, birds of a feather flock together!"

"And are you?"

"A blot? Yes, if you want to get technical! I'm the black sheep of the family. Dad made me drop out of the university; said he wasn't going to throw good money after bad. I didn't care, I hated it. So now I work awhile here and there, at whatever I can get. I'd just had all I could stand of trying to live my life to suit dad's plans. He wanted me to be a music major and find some nice young minister to marry--- I have neither the talent nor the desire to do either!"

"I can certainly understand. But I do want you to come with me, unless you'd rather not attend at all."

"It'll be a kick---set the old fogies on their ears! Now, I want to know if there is someone special in your life!"

"No. I dated now and then. Just when I'd think we were getting along fine he'd blow the whole thing."

"Now what happened, I want to hear this!"

"Well, we'd be out having a nice time---a movie and a

quick bite afterward. Then later we'd talk a while, I'd be going on about something and he'd just grab me---right out of the blue---breathing all over me---it was disgusting---happened with every guy! Needless to say, I had few second dates!"

Rachel was trying not to laugh. "So, you haven't changed! You're still a prude and I'm glad of it! John will be too! You know, you are the only girl he talks about, or ever did for that matter. He and I are still close, I'm happy to say, in spite of dad."

"Good. How are things with John, what's he doing now?"

"I forget how far behind you are, Ellen! John did what dad wanted, he's been a combined assistant pastor and youth minister at the church. But now that dad's retired John is full time there. Dad still tries to hold the reins; he tries to pressure John to preach his way. But John does his own sermons, although he tries never to upset dad. Dad isn't well, or so he claims, I'm not sure I believe him---says his heart is bad and I'm sure he blames me for that! He's an impossible old goat!"

"What about your mother, how is she?"

"oh, she's fine. I don't know how she stands staying in that house all day with dad, waiting on him for every little thing I really think she gets some kind of pleasure from his dependency---I find it all so depressing!" She shook her head as if to rid herself of her thoughts. "But John would love to see you, he'd be hurt if I didn't let him know immediately that you're back. Let's run out there, can you get away?"

"Sure, I've closed the shop, I'm getting ready to re-do it."

"I wondered why it was locked, is it all up to you---you can decide everything?"

"Yes---Megan just sent me up here and turned me loose! It's been running in the red, so now I'm to bring it around and make it show a profit! I'm really excited about it!"

"Kind of a scary thing, isn't it?"

"It is, if I think about it too much! But I'll just do things the way Megan does. If I pattern it after Paige's in Wilmington I can't go wrong!"

"Megan's shop there is all that successful?"

"Rachel, you'd love it---it's larger than this, of course, with different rooms, each with a separate name---"

"Sounds a lot more posh than I'm used to, I've never even bought anything here!"

"I can see why not, there's nothing very inviting about this place."

"Ellen, what are you going to wear to the party?" Rachel went to a dress rack and restlessly flipped through the smaller sizes.

"I don't know, I didn't bring much with me. Thought I'd get some things here. Why don't we both look through and see what we like, it'd be fun---but we've got all week, since the shop's closed we can do it anytime."

"Fine with me! Let's go see John now, I'll call to be sure he's at the church. You do have a car?"

"Yes." I watched Rachel as she made the call. She was truly a beautiful young woman, her black hair was long and thick, tumbling about her face with a careless charm. Her crystal-blue eyes were bright with anticipation when she hung up.

"Would you mind driving, Rachel? I want to enjoy the scenery."

She reached for the keys. "Sure, I don't see what there is to enjoy, but we always were silly over the opposite things!"

"Oh, not always---I used to have a crush on Rex Post the time you did, I just didn't tell you!"

Rachel looked at me oddly, "Really? I trust you've gotten over it?" She swung the car into thickening traffic.

"Oh, long ago! Didn't you?"

"No. Wish I had---I've put in more time and energy trying to get him to marry me than anything else in my life! But I think Rex loves me, or at least most of the time I do!"

"Then what's stopping him?" I was watching her profile. There was a sort of sultry sophistication about

Rachel, she didn't have to cultivate it---I doubted that she was even aware of it but it made the little-girl hurt in her voice all the more touching.

"Ellen, I don't understand---I thought if I let Rex know how I feel about him, it would change him---and when we're together it's great, but then I don't see him for a couple of weeks or longer. Then he just drops in, so sure I'll be waiting for him---and I am!"

I cleared my throat, "Maybe it's money. Can he afford marriage?"

"That isn't it. He's always got money to spend and more ways of getting it than I know about. Right now, he's paying my rent. I'm broke, no job---none in sight! So now you know what I've been doing all these years---nothing!" She grinned and I thought how she really hadn't changed--- she always could cry one minute and laugh the next!

"Rachel, you know I'll be hoping for you. I'm happy with what I'm doing, and I want you to be happy, too."

"You're not shocked---a minister's daughter living such an irresponsible life?"

"I just hope you and Rex can work things out."

She gave me a quick look and for a second, I saw something calculating in her eyes. Or I thought I did--- perhaps the subject was making us both uneasy.

"Does John live with your parents?"

"Oh, yes, dad wouldn't have it any other way---and it is handy for John, the poor guy!"

"Why do you say that? Has something happened to him?"

"No, he's fine, physically---but you can imagine his position, a single, young minister---every woman in the church who has even a half grown daughter keeps shoving the poor things at him---he has a constant parade to his door of pies, cakes, and cookies!"

"I see! Most men wouldn't be too offended by all that attention, I shouldn't think. Isn't there anyone John's interested in?"

"No, and it makes him so uncomfortable he has a hard time trying to handle the situation---especially since dad pushes him to hurry up and get married! Dad says John would win the total trust of the congregation so much quicker if he were married. You know, ministers often do a certain amount of counseling, marital problems and all that. Much as I hate to admit it, dad probably has a point, and I think John knows it too."

"A touchy spot for John! I hate to hear that, I don't know a kinder, more dear person than John. I've wondered about him often, hoping he was happy."

"Have you really, Ellen?" Rachel flicked me a quick look.

"Of course. John always treated me the way I supposed an older brother would if I'd had one---and I guess I thought of him as a brother, we always got along well"

"That's true, you did." There was a little smile in her voice. "I'm glad John is doing some work in the church office, that's best."

"Why?" the drive had seemed short, and now Rachel pulled up close to the small brick church.

"John's always more himself away from the folks, this way you'll see how glad he'll really be to have you back! Oh, Ellen, I didn't tell him on the phone why I was coming--- you're a surprise!"

I had to laugh at Rachel's delight. Beneath all her unhappiness she was the same mischievous girl, and I was glad of it! I had to run to catch up with her and it was like old times as she eased open a side door and tiptoed down a hall to the office door.

"Wait here." Rachel opened the door. "Here I am, John!"

"What's up, Sis? You sounded a bit odd when you called."

I couldn't see John from where I stood, but his voice was familiar though much more mature than when I'd last heard it---and with something in it that told me he was used to hearing mostly bad news from Rachel.

"Go ahead with what you're doing, looks as if you're nearly finished. I only need a moment of your time---" Rachel motioned for me to enter and I silently came to stand

21

beside her. John's back was toward us. He was quite tall, like his parents, but while I remembered them as being thin, John was muscular.

"Hurry up, John, I'm tired of waiting!"

"Rachel, you are the most---" John's voice broke off as he swung around to face us. "Ellen?" His eyes were bluer than I'd remembered, a clear, startling blue that softened with his smile.

I stepped toward him; my hand outstretched. Still he stared at me, as if he needed to double-check my identity. Then before I knew he was moving, he was across the room and I was clasped against him in a bear hug that left me breathless! "Ellen!"

"You said that already, John." Rachel was pretending impatience, but I knew she had thoroughly enjoyed his reaction.

John released me and we both sat down on straight backed chairs. "Ellen, I can't believe you're here---just the other day Rachel and I were talking about you, wondering how things were going with you! Sit down, Sis! We three have some catching up to do!"

"No, thanks, John. I'll go over and tell Mom we're here." Rachel smiled at us and I thought she looked very pleased. I looked at John. Alone, we were strangely silent.

"I'm going to replace these chairs soon."

"You should. They remind me of the ones in your mother's dining room---too hard for comfort!"

"You just didn't like sitting still for long---how about now, are you back to stay?"

"I think so. If all goes well."

"You've seen your father, haven't you?"

"Yes. Yesterday when I arrived---I couldn't wait to see Fox Hollow,"

"I thought not---how did it go, seeing your father after so long?"

"Not good, not bad, I guess." I answered him frankly. It would not have occurred to me to be anything less with John. "I really didn't expect much of a welcome from him."

"Then what has happened that you didn't expect---

something has taken the wind out of your sails!" He was leaning toward me, elbows propped on his knees and his large hands clasped.

I shrugged and met his gaze. John was a very perceptive person and I quickly wondered if this same sensitivity might not work against him in his relationship with his father.

"I'm waiting, Ellen, might as well 'fess up."

"There is something---it'll probably sound really silly, saying it out loud, in the daylight---at least, I hope it does---" I told him about the phone call to my motel room, sounding as off-hand about it as I could. "---I'm sure it was either Bertha or someone she put up to doing it."

"Where are you staying tonight?"

"Well, I don't know yet, but I'll get a room when we're back in town. I hope to find an apartment soon."

"I'd ask you to stay with us, but I know you wouldn't be comfortable around my parents."

"Thank you, but I'll manage fine. I'm sure it won't happen again. Bertha should have it out of her system by now. I'm afraid I made her mad yesterday, and she doesn't like the idea of my being back here. I think she's worried I'll move in at Fox Hollow and upset the way she runs things."

"If that's all there is to it, I'm sure you're right. But call me if it happens again---I want to keep an eye on you."

"I will. Enough about that! John, I'm very proud of you, you're doing something so worthwhile." I walked to his desk. "Is this what you're working on? I picked up a sheet of paper, across the top was printed: SATAN'S FIB + ADAM'S RIB − WOMAN'S LIB.

"John---is this your sermon?" I was surprised at the implications of the title, and disappointed.

He took the paper from me. "It's one of father's, one he didn't get to deliver before his health forced him to retire. I was reading it, but I'm not going use it."

"I'm glad---if it's anything like the title suggests!"

"People here were used to his sermons, but this one is quite biased, you're right about that. His sermons were becoming more so all the time."

"Because of me---right, John?" Rachel had entered without our knowing, purposely, I suspected.

"Sis, let it go---he isn't well, hasn't been for some time---he's a harmless old man."

"Harmless? Maybe the day he dies, maybe not even then! But Ellen knows how he used to be, she can probably imagine how it's been since."

For the first time I felt uncomfortable with Rachel and John. "Should I go over and say hello, or is this a bad time?"

"Mom did say dad had a restless morning, so another time would be better. We'll come back out soon. Mom said to tell you she's glad you're back."

If that's so, she's certainly changed, I thought. Aloud I said, "We should go, Rachel, I'm sure we're keeping John from his work. The annual party at Fox Hollow is this Saturday, John, are you going---or do you ever attend---I don't know if it's considered a proper place for a minister to be or not!"

John laughed and for a moment he was transformed---I knew then what I hadn't been able to put my finger on before. He had seemed so much older than I knew him to be, there was that air of weariness about him---but, for the moment, it lifted.

"I'll come for a while; I won't stay long. I'd either put a damper on the evening for most of the guests or they wouldn't want to face me on Sunday morning! Are you going Rachel?"

"Oh, yes, Ellen and I are escorting each other---we wouldn't miss it! So we'll see you Saturday if not before."

He walked us to the door and waved us off. He was still standing there when I looked back.

"Well, Ellen, what do you think of John?"

"I'm impressed, and proud of him, and I told him so. But I'm not nearly as proud as you are!"

Rachel grinned, "You can tell?" You're right---I'm proud of him, and I love him, he's always stood by me as much as he possibly could!"

"He's certainly a handsome man! I can understand the young ladies in the church wanting to bake him cookies!

"He's a hunk, alright! And wasn't it fun---surprising him like that! Didn't I tell you he's be glad to see you?"

"It was quite a welcome, good thing I'm a quick healer! He gave my ribs some squeeze."

"Ellen, that's the first time I've ever seen John react so---well, for John, that was downright uninhibited!"

"Now Rachel, "I laughed, "you ae not going to get me to blush over John! I recall very well how you used to do that every chance you got---how you tried to get us together!"

"I was kind of bad about that, I admit! Then my parents would never have allowed it---now they'd both welcome you with open arms!"

"What!" I croaked the word. Rachel's face was serious now as she watched the road.

"It's true. Dad is desperate for John to marry! I told mom how John acted when he saw you, she was so pleased she couldn't hide it."

"Oh, come on now, Rachel! No guy who looks like that has any trouble attracting girls---you said yourself they're standing in line! What are you trying to hand me, anyway?

"It's very involved---maybe we'll discuss it another time. I think I'm too protective toward John, it's hard to explain---but Ellen, you can believe me when I say that if he ever marries, the one he chooses had better make him happy---I'd kill anyone who'd hurt him in any way!"

As I stared at Rachel's stony face, I realized I believed her, at least for the moment! I felt as if I'd received a warning.

Rachel pulled up in front of an apartment complex. "Not much, but it's home, for now anyway."

The modest buildings were in need of repair. Paint was peeling off the doors and some of the apartment numbers were missing.

I slid under the wheel as she got out, "I know you'll be busy Ellen, but call me when you can, I'm usually free---and welcome back!"

I watched her walk away. I was surprised at the turn Rachel's life had taken, but I was sure her father had given her little choice. He was certainly not the type to welcome her home again after taking her out of the university. If I could help her, I would, I decided. Then I turned my attention to my own problems.

Three

As soon as I was settled in a different motel, I drove to a drive-in restaurant and ordered a sandwich to take back to the shop. In the office I cleared the cluttered desk and sat in the swivel chair---at least it was comfortable. I was sure there would be many more meals eaten at this desk.

I thought of the day, nearly three weeks ago now, when Megan had rather cautiously approached the subject of the shop. She had just finished a painting and smelled of the turpentine she used in cleaning her brushes. In her old jeans and sweatshirt, she had looked a far cry from one of Wilmington's most successful businesswomen.

She had said, "Ellen, I have to admit I've made a big mistake keeping Mrs. Birkdale on. We need new ideas, new lines---we've got to bring that shop up with the times! It's been an expensive lesson and will become even more so if we don't do something soon."

"Mrs. Birkdale is wanting to retire, so this is a good

time to make a decision. Are you thinking of selling?"

"No, at least not yet---there's money to be made there, I'm sure. How would you feel about going back to Indiana? I'd give you a free hand with the shop---anything at all you felt would improve it you'd be free to do!"

I'd felt a swift surge of excitement. "Do you want me to go back?"

"I want you happy---that's all I've ever wanted, even before you came to live with me! I've loved having you here. This past year has been the best of all, I really enjoyed all our buying trips. You've been a real help to me, Ellen, you've done a good job with everything I've entrusted to you. But you've prepared yourself for a career of your own---" she was quiet a moment, regarding me intently, "---think about it, but make the choice for yourself, with your own wishes in mind."

"The first thing I'll do is change the name. The Vogue is a bit stuffy---your shop here is Paige's, why not call it Paige Two? And if it needs redecorating, it'll get it---still want me to manage it?"

"That was quick! But don't go back just because you feel it will please me."

"Aunt Meg, you've always known what I needed, and I do want to do something on my own, especially something for you, I owe you so much! We both know where I'd be by now if I hadn't had you to turn to."

She had kissed my cheek, "Ellen, you owe me nothing, don't ever think you do!" And for just a moment, I'd thought there was something else she wanted to say but she'd just patted my shoulder and left the room.

Now---here I was! I had thought about it long before Megan brought it up. I had known the shop was not doing what she had expected, and I'd welcomed the challenge---I more than welcomed it, I relished the whole situation! It was the answer to everything. I could help Megan and, at the same time, fulfill a desire that I knew had grown out of all proportion throughout the year---I could show my father I had a purpose in life other than that of a brood mare! I'd be just as successful in my way as he had been in his---but he could not see it if I was in North Carolina, I'd have to prove it in Indiana---and now I had the chance!

And---there was Mitch Kramer---I couldn't deny he was the cause of some of the excitement I felt. I'd kept a memory of him that was foolishly unchanged, but I couldn't alter it---I had no way of knowing what the years had changed about him, or if he even remembered me, but somehow I'd never doubted that he would still be here when I came back to Fox Hollow.

There had been very little contact with my father. Three years ago, he had condescended to invite Megan and me to come for a visit during the last of April. The "Farmer's Ball", as he so disdainfully called it, would be held at that time and he had thought Megan might find it amusing. The party was in appreciation of those neighbors who allowed, however begrudgingly, father's hunts to continue onto their land when it was necessary. But on the day of the festivities, all malice was put aside and everyone who had had the slightest connection with Fox hollow throughout the year showed up for the party. This was always foreseen and there was a banquet that would impress and warm, at least temporarily, father's coolest critics while the entire evening a band from Indianapolis or perhaps Terre Haute would play until daybreak, if anyone was still there to hear.

Megan had declined the invitation, and the one the following spring. This spring there had been no invitation, for my father was too proud, I knew, to risk another refusal.

But I was here, and I would attend! Would I see Mitch? I had not asked Rachel about him; she would have known he was important to me and I was not ready to share that with anyone.

I reached for the phone and dialed Rachel's apartment. I suddenly wanted company.

"Rachel---if you aren't busy can you come to the shop?"

"Sure! I'm bored stiff here---I wanted to come anyway but I was afraid I'd keep you from your work. I'll be right there!"

An idea had formed almost as we talked. If she would

be interested, Rachel could be of real help to me. I jumped
when the phone rang---I hoped it wasn't Bertha making one
of her calls again!

"The Vogue, good afternoon."

"Is this Miss Jordane?" The voice was a bit impatient.

"Yes, it is."

"I'm Trudy Porter, you don't know me, but I help at
the shop on Fridays and Saturdays."

"Yes, Mrs. Birkdale told me."

"Well, I understand you're closing the shop to make
some changes. Now I can't wait that long to come back to
work, I've ordered new carpet all through the house, wall to
wall, and my husband says it's up to me to pay for it! I've got
the chance to get on at a factory full time and I'm just going
to have to take it! Really, I was needing to switch anyway---
part time in a dress shop just doesn't pay many bills, if you
know what I mean! No hard feelings, I hope, Miss Jordane,
but that's just how it's got to be!"

"I understand, Mrs. Porter, good luck in your new
position." As I hung up I had to smile. What a pair Trudy
and Mrs. Birkdale must have been! I was anxious for Rachel
to arrive. There was a staggering amount of work ahead, but
I would need help and Rachel could be the solution.

Finally, she tapped on the door and I hurried to let her
in. "I've something to ask you, Rachel, and I'll get right to
the point. Would you consider working here?"

"Ellen! I don't know anything about expensive
clothes---I certainly don't own any---I couldn't even dress
nicely enough to work here!"

"Rachel, clothes are no problem. You'd be welcome to
take some things from the shop---it'd be great
advertisement; your figure would sell anything you put on!
And by the time we took inventory and inspected new
shipments for flaws and steamed the wrinkles out, you'd
know every item and every brand name by heart!"

"But Ellen---what about the customers---I don't know
how to handle people, I've never had to!"

"That's the easy part! You know how you like to be
treated when you shop, just treat them the same way! It

doesn't take long to find which customers appreciate your suggestions and which ones prefer to be left alone. We'll both be feeling our way in that area, as I'll know none of the regular customers---if there are any!"

"I certainly need a job---and I love nice clothes, and I'd love working with you---so---yes!"

"Wonderful! Let's go in the back and I'll see what I can offer you in the way of salary. I'm sure I can raise it later, but just let me check these records a minute and I'll know where I can start you."

I had not yet checked to see what Mrs. Birkdale paid Trudy Porter, but I wanted Rachel and I intended to pay her a salary that would keep her interested. I had not forgotten the way she used to sidestep trouble with her father when we were children. If she used half as much tact with the demanding clientele a shop such as this attracted, she would be invaluable.

I circled a figure and handed it to Rachel. "Is this agreeable, at least for the time being?"

"Ellen---do you know this means I can pay my own rent?" She laughed and I felt good at her reaction.

"Then let's do something to celebrate---let's choose what we want to wear Saturday night! Anything at all---it's yours!"

Like two little girls playing dress-up, we tried on everything that held the slightest bit of promise and several things that held none, laughing at the sometimes-outrageous results.

"Rachel, some of this has definitely got to go! When we reopen, we'll have a terrific sale---it'll draw people in to see the new merchandise!"

"I haven't been this excited in years---Miss Ellen Paige Jordane has been in town a mere twenty four hours and already she's changed my life---what if you'd never left, Ellen, what would these past years have been like?"

Rachel stood beside me and we stared at our reflections in the triple mirror. She was not as tall as I, but she was perfectly proportioned---the gown she wore had looked deceivingly demur on its hanger, now it looked twice its price.

"It's for certain we wouldn't be having all this fun! As for me, had things not changed as drastically as they did, father would no doubt have had his way and I'd be living at Fox Hollow, married to the first guy he could rope into it, raising who knows how many grandsons---and going quietly crazy the way my mother did!"

"Ugh! What a picture! Guess we'll just say things turned out for the best and let it go at that! What do you think, should I wear this Saturday night?"

"It looks super, Rachel! It just depends on how you want to spend your evening---think you'll be up to fighting the fellows off all night?"

"Well, to tell the truth, I'm just interested in one fellow. I want to see Rex green with jealousy!"

"Then that gown should do it. But if Rex is going, wouldn't you rather go with him? I won't mind."

"Rex will be there, you can count on it, but he didn't ask me---he likes his freedom. He won't even expect me to be there---I'm fed up with his attitude, things are going to change!"

"What does Rex do, Rachel, for a job, I mean?"

She went into a dressing room. "He owns his parents' grocery; you remember that little country store? They died some time ago. Rex has some things going on the side, but he doesn't talk about them, so I don't really know what he's involved in."

"Then he didn't go ahead and become a veterinarian?"

"Hardly! He gave that up quick enough---too much hard work for him! He always wanted the easy money, and he's still looking for it!" She came out, her arms full of dresses. "I have no high ideals where Rex is concerned, Ellen, I know him for what he is! I just know I want him, and I think he is the second thing I'd kill for." There was no smile as she went to hang the gowns in place.

"Well! Let me declare myself right now---I have not the slightest romantic interest in Rex---I'm just interested in whether he makes you happy or unhappy!"

"We'll just get busy and find you someone, Ellen. I

have a feeling we won't have to look far!"

"Don't worry about me, Rachel, I'm the prude, remember? Now, I'll be here by eight o'clock in the morning. You don't have to come in that early, but I've got a lot of book work to do. Here's your key. And take that gown with you if you've decided on it."

"Thank you, Ellen, for the job and the gown! You can't know how much it means to me. I'm going home and call John, I can't wait to tell him!"

The shop seemed oddly still and empty. Rachel's presence had had its effect on it, and on me. Even though our friendship seemed unchanged, still she had shown a side of herself that was bitter and ready to attack anyone she considered a threat to the attainment of what she wanted. In this case, it was Rex. Her pursuit of him seemed to me to be almost desperate. So unnecessary for someone like Rachel, the girl I remembered deserved much more than that.

The rest of the week whirled past---Rachel took inventory while I studied the record books and decorating estimates. I was relieved to find no problem with Mrs. Birkdale's methods, where the bookwork was concerned, she had been very capable. The only trouble, it seemed, centered around drawing customers and keeping them for repeat sales, and I was sure I could remedy that.

On Saturday we worked until noon, then walked in the warm sunshine to the nearest restaurant for lunch.

"Rachel, I feel as if we've been cooped up in that shop for weeks!"

"Tonight will change that! We've worked hard, we deserve to have a night out!"

"We will, at that. We've got things in good shape for the painters on Monday. I'm glad things are moving so quickly."

"You aren't eating, Ellen. Are you nervous about tonight?"

"I hate to admit that I am! I'm glad John is going with us, you two may be the only friends I have there. I'm sure father will do or say something to make me uncomfortable!"

"Let's see, who's apt to be there you'll know---Rex, of

course, and there's a guy Rex knows, Mitch Kramer---but you knew him, you must remember all the times he was at the house to see John and Rex? Rex and Mitch were friends when they were freshmen at IU, and, although Rex left school and Mitch transferred to a school in Illinois, they saw each other during the summers. But there will be old neighbors, and kids we went to grade school and junior high with."

I took a deep breath. "I remember Mitch, he was always very nice, I thought."

"Oh, really? Well, good---he's with the forestry now, does a lot of---whatever the forestry does---here at Monroe Reservoir. Say, you don't know about that, do you? It's huge, practically an inland sea, even gets white-caps when it gets stormy. You'll have to get John to drive you out there."

I glanced at her, she seemed never to miss a chance to mention John. "Rachel, I'm just not hungry. Are you?"

"I'm ready to go, I have to, in fact---have to get my hair done."

"I'll come by for you early enough that we'll have time to talk to your mother when we stop for John."

"I'll be ready, Ellen. But isn't it odd, here you are attending this party as a guest, when if things had gone to suit your father, you'd be acting as hostess tonight!"

"Bertha is welcome to that job, I assume she'll be there in that capacity, clucking all around! It'll be interesting, I'm sure!"

Rachel laughed and waved as she left. She was full of anticipation while I was becoming more nervous as the day went on. I would have to contend with my father and Bertha, two totally unpredictable people and neither of them happy to see me! And if Mitch should be at the party, I had no assurance he would even remember me, certainly not as I remembered him.

Never had I taken such pain with my appearance---I soaked in a tub piled high with bubbles instead of the usual quick shower. I had decided against having my hair done, now I was sorry. My casual style no longer pleased me. I applied my makeup with great care and was pleased to note I had not yet lost my tan. North Carolina had been well into spring before I left, and Megan and I had spent the weekends strolling the beach.

Again, I checked my hair. I wore it brushed back from my face and it fell to my shoulders with just a bit of curve at the ends that kept it from looking too severe. It would have to do; I didn't want my father to think I had gone to any special effort for this party.

I put on the dress I had finally chosen, a sea-green gown with a halter top, tight fitting midriff and a full skirt that floated when I moved. I looked in the mirror, a little surprised. The overall effect was just right, I decided The dress was simply cut, relying on the fabric to carry it, the color set off my tan and deepened my auburn hair---I looked, yes---willowy, and soft and romantic! Yet, the moment I stepped away from the mirror I was again uncertain.

I pulled up to Rachel's door, hoping she was watching for me. She came out immediately. I caught my breath---she was stunning. Her black hair was done up on her head in soft curls with a few wispy tendrils against the nape of her neck.

"Rachel, you are beautiful! Rex will be putty in your hands!"

"You think so? I gave it my best shot! You look great, that's a good color for you."

"Thanks, but we're in different leagues! I hope John doesn't have a call at the last minute, I'm sure that's a hazard in his work."

"He'll not miss this, come hell or high water! And neither would I, I'm glad you asked me."

"Rex still doesn't know you're coming?"

"No, and I'm going to love it! He doesn't think I've got the nerve to face these people, seeing as most of them attend the church and heard dad's public denouncement of me!"

"He made a public statement about you?"

"Oh, yes---he didn't want anyone to think he was too proud to confess he'd failed with me. Pride is a deadly sin and all that!"

"Rachel, I can't believe it! I don't know whose father

is the hardest to take; yours or mine! But I'm glad you're with me, I wouldn't want to be without your support tonight, or John's! We'll just concentrate on enjoying the evening, our father's attitudes are their problem, not ours!'

Rachel smiled agreement. We were well out of town and winding deep into the countryside. The soft evening air erased the last trace of our unhappy thoughts and I found the scenic drive was having a calming effect that I very much needed.

We passed the church and a few yards beyond was the Flagg's home. I parked the car.

"Mom is anxious to see you, Ellen, especially all done up for the party. Dad never would attend, much as she wanted to. I know he'd throw a fit at John's going if he knew!"

Reluctantly, I followed Rachel inside. It was so strange to be back in this house. I was trying not to slip backward into the old feelings the Flagg's always evoked. I knew I would be more thoroughly inspected tonight than ever before. It was like stepping into the past, even the furniture was arranged much as I remembered it!

Opal Flagg came toward us. She was thin to the point of gauntness. "Ellen, welcome back! Oh, you girls look lovely! It's been such a long time, Ellen, we hope you're here to stay. Sit down and talk to me. Rachel will have to go over to the church and get John, he never knows what time it is."

Without a word Rachel left the room, leaving me to wonder why she didn't just use the phone. I settled on the edge of a chair.

"As I said, Ellen, we three are happy you're here. I haven't mentioned that you're back to the Reverend. We don't always tell him everything these days, as he is so often confused---I'm sure Rachel told you of his condition."

I nodded, "She mentioned he had some health problems." My voice sounded as strained as I felt.
"Oh, it's more than physical, I'm afraid, he goes off on real tangents sometimes---usually about John---and we have a hard time calming him."

I was pinned by her large luminous eyes. I resisted

the urge to squirm in my chair---I was not a child and I would not be made to feel like one! The silence hung between us---she seemed to expect some reply.

"But I'm sure you both are very pleased with John's decision to work in the ministry---and it must be a comfort, having him here with you."

"Yes, of course, but the Reverend has the dream of seeing John marry and start a family. He's afraid he'll die before that happens and sometimes it bears on his mind so heavily it brings on a bad spell. That's especially hard on John, as he feels so responsible where his father is concerned---"

"Opal!"

I jumped---I had assumed that Reverend Flagg was sleeping. His voice still held its demanding tone---as if he did not expect to have to call again. To my surprise, Mrs. Flagg went smoothly on.

"---Rachel and I try to assure John that the Reverend's condition is in no way his fault, but John takes his father's wishes so to heart---always has!"

"Opal!"

There was a threatening note to the Reverend's voice this time, and I was certain Mrs. Flagg would hurry to his bedside. But she showed not the slightest sign of having heard him. I wondered if perhaps her hearing was poor, if I should tell her he was calling. I was becoming more uncomfortable all the time---where was that Rachel!

"Opal?"

Now there was a quiver in his voice, a questioning. I saw the small hint of a smile cross Mrs. Flagg's face.

"Excuse me, Ellen." She went quickly out of the room.

I leaned back and let out my breath. She had looked pleased for just an instant---now I knew she had heard him each time, but she would not answer until he had begun to doubt that she was there. It seemed a cruel thing to do, even to him.

"Where's mom?"

"She's in with your father, Rachel. I was about to wait for you outside.

John spoke rather roughly, "Sis, you shouldn't have left Ellen waiting in here. You two go on to the car, I'll look in on them and be right out. Ellen," he turned to face me, "you look lovely!"

Rachel shrugged and followed me outside." John's right, but I'm so used to those two I forget how it might seem to others. I'm afraid I only have Rex on my mind!"

"Don't worry about it. I didn't find it all that bad. But I did see how things are with your parents, your mother is--- not the way I remember her!"

"I know. Actually, I wanted you to see how things are, it will help you understand John."

I looked at her in surprise. What did she mean by that, why should I need to understand anything about her brother---I had no time to ask, for just then John slid into the driver's seat.

Driving away from the house, their moods suddenly changed. Rachel was excited and John was back in good humor.

"How will you get home, John? I'm sure Ellen and I will stay longer than you plan to"

"No problem---I'll take shank's mare! I enjoy walking, anytime of day or night. How many times would you say you walked this road between our houses, Ellen?

"I couldn't guess! But I may be ready to leave early myself, so don't take off without checking with me."

Rachel's voice was as patient as if she was explaining to ta child. "Now Ellen, we'll keep an eye on you! But John is the one who'll be in need of rescue---you'll see what I mean about the young ladies hereabout! As for myself, Rex will be most anxious to take me home---or I'll know the reason why!"

It was already deep dusk as we drove through the gates of Fox Hollow At the top of the hill I wanted to ask John to stop a moment, so breathtaking was the sight of the big house below, ablaze with light and glittering like a jewel stitched into the velvet twilight. I felt the unexpected sting of tears---I loved this place with all my heart.

As if John knew my feelings, he slowed the car as we

neared the crest of the drive. Then, in what seemed the very next second, we were walking toward the house---this was Fox Hollow in all its glory---my Fox Hollow!

Four

The long porch curving around three sides of the house was balanced in light and shadows, for each supporting post held two glowing lanterns, leaving the sections of porch in between invitingly dim. Light from inside the house illumined the stained-glass window in the massive front door, making each color vibrant.

Inside we were met by a maid who took our wraps. John arched an eyebrow at me and I felt oddly embarrassed at father's bit of pretentiousness. Rachel had hurried on in, to look for Rex, I was sure. John and I trailed behind, taking it all in.

Mirrors ran the length of the huge room, reflecting the gleam of big brass bowls filled with flowers. Even the ornate walnut woodwork had been rubbed to a sheen. Additional furniture had arrived since my first visit and had been placed in ways to provide intimate seating for either couples or groups.

"Ellen, this is impressive---but I suppose you were used to all this when you were still at home."

"I was not allowed to attend the parties. Children are never included---this is really my first post-season party!"

"Then this is a first for both of us. Say, are you hungry?"

I shook my head, "Not really."

"Well, I am! And I know you were too nervous to eat lunch, Rachel told me---where is she, anyway?"

"Looking for me?" Rachel appeared beside us. Rex isn't here yet, but some friends I haven't seen in ages asked me to join them. I'm sure you two won't miss me! Come around after awhile and I'll introduce you, Ellen." And with that she melted away into the crowd.

John shook his head and grinned, "I'm sorry, Ellen. Rachel is as obvious as ever! She always had you picked out for me!"

"Oh, I know---just let her play her game, she enjoys it! It doesn't bother me."

He offered his arm and we walked out across the hall into the dining room. There was a long line of people around the table, laughing and talking as they chose from the sumptuous fare.

That my father opened his home this way every year had always surprised me, because I knew all too well how far above his neighbors, he considered himself! But it paid off, I was sure, or he would not have continued the practice---plus it gave him the chance to show his house and possessions--- my father was a man who needed to feel he was admired, or even more to his liking---envied.

I looked at faces, some were familiar and I returned their smiles while I searched the room for Mitch---would he be here---would he be happy to see me, or would he even care?

Gradually I began to notice several of the women were making an extra effort to file past John and myself. Some were near my age, most were younger, often with an overzealous mother at her side. John introduced me, but I was not given the same warm smile they bestowed upon him.

When the procession ended, I whispered to John, "Well! Rachel wasn't kidding---you do need protection!"

To my delight he blushed and I thought how marvelously unchanged he was, that he did indeed deserve the perfect wife Rachel so wanted for him.

"Ellen, I want to tell you how much I appreciate what you've done for Rachel. This job means a lot to her---and to me! She won't have to rely on Rex Post for anything---I wish she'd forget him entirely!"

Before I could reply, Bertha sailed into the room, making her way through the people as an ocean liner parts the sea. She wore a dress of pink chiffon, its long skirt billowing out around her. Three long strands of crystal beads caught the light as she moved, seeming to flash a desperate S. O. S. just before they plunged over the ruffles undulating down the front of her dress. Bertha's short, brown hair had been curled too tightly, leaving uneven clumps around her head. But what I thought she'd feel was the most fashionable touch of all was the rhinestone tiara perched atop her tightly wadded hair!

I spoke low, "Oh, John! Isn't she a sad sight!"

"That's a charitable observation, after the way she's always treated you! Especially since you suspect she was behind that phone call---I take it you've not been bothered again?"

"No. I've put it out of my mind. I've been too busy to think about it. It's hard to take Bertha seriously at all the way she looks tonight, much less to think of her as a threat! She's decked out like the Queen Mary!"

"Maybe I bragged on you too soon!"

"That did sound mean, I know, but I'm curious--- someone here has shown good taste---the furniture is lovely, and this food---"

John had taken advantage of a break in the line and we were trying to choose from the endless array of tempting dishes.

"Looks good, don't it? Bertha had moved into line

beside us.

"Yes, Bertha, everything looks lovely. You have really worked hard to make this a success." I hoped if I admitted that much she would move on.

"Nope! I ain't hardly done nothin'---ain't like it used to be when Claudette was runnin' the show---I don't stay in the kitchen sweatin' and cookin' all hours of the day and night! Got this all catered! Been doin' it this way the past few years. Things have changed, and I like it this way!"

Bertha turned to John. "Glad you came, the old Reverend never did! Bet you there's plenty of gals disappointed you didn't bring them instead of Ellen---lots of these women would be after you their selves if you wasn't a bit too young for them!" She poked her elbow in John's side and laughed, making her tiara wobble.

"Where is father? We haven't seen him tonight." I was not really interested, but I hoped to spare John further embarrassment.

"Why, he's minglin' with folks, wants to be sure everyone's havin' fun! She grinned widely and winked in the old way I remembered, then turning her attention to the people around us she smiled and nodded her way across the room. She was basking in her triumph, which was obviously what she considered this evening to be---she was making certain I understood there was no room for me at Fox Hollow!

John and I carried our plates of food outside and found an empty corner on the far end of the porch. "Ellen, I'll get your wrap, it may be a bit cool out here for you."

I watched him make his way back inside. He is a very handsome man---I waited, but no stir of feeling followed the thought---sorry, Rachel, but I'm not the one for John! I was the one for Mitch---even though he didn't know it, I did!

Waiting, I breathed in the tantalizing fragrance of honey-suckle on the night air. It was quite dark now, the moon was climbing above the ridge of trees that edged the hills. Couples would be sure to take advantage of its light and steal away from the crowd---I felt an empty surge of loneliness, much like the feeling that had drawn me back to

Fox Hollow. But now I was back and there was no reason to feel sad---I had the shop to occupy my time; that alone was an exciting prospect---

Then John was suddenly at my side, his face a mixture of anxiety and impatience. The impatience, I could see, was aimed at Rachel, whom he had in tow. She shrugged her shoulders in resignation.

"Tell her, John, she'll get used to it if she goes anywhere with you very often! You're the one who thinks we should go---so explain to Ellen!"

"Mother only called when she was certain it was necessary---we can hardly leave her to deal with father alone!" He turned to me. "Ellen, there was a call while I was inside, father has taken a bad turn---"

"I am sorry, John, but go, you and Rachel hurry on home and don't worry about me! Take my car, you have the keys. I'll use one of father's."

John hurried down the porch steps. Rachel seemed in no rush at all , and to my surprise she linger behind.

"Ellen, if you see Rex, tell him what happened. I'll see you at the shop Monday morning."

"Rachel, you needn't come in, your mother may need you---even if your father pulls through this!"

"Oh, he'll pull through, he always does! I think he times these little spells to coincide with the social events John attend, they never seem to happen when John is busy with church business. Makes you wonder, doesn't it?"

She sauntered off, making John wait. I stared after them. How strange their lives were, still totally influenced by their father---but with my second thought, I realized I as in much the same situation.

The food on my plate had no appeal now, and I carried what I could safely balance to the kitchen. Bertha was watching a maid arrange a tray of elegant desserts. She saw me put down the plates of untouched food.

"What's the matter? Ain't it as good as you're used to?" A dark flush had swept up to Bertha's fuzzy hair, as if the pink ruffles were suddenly choking her. I was startled at the venom in her voice.

"I'm sure it's delicious, but I've lost my appetite and John had no chance to enjoy his meal at all---" I went on to tell her what had happened.

"The old Reverend likes to keep them jumpin'---John is the only one who really takes him seriously, he never seem to catch on!" She was staring at me. "You're all growed up now, sure a different lookin' girl than when you left! But such a long time makes changes---made some around here you can bet!

"I know, Bertha, and I'm not here to interfere with the way you run Fox Hollow---I've enough to do, I assure you." I turned and left the kitchen before she could answer. I felt tired and drained and was ready to borrow a car and leave.

But in the hall father met me and with an exuberance that stunned me, he whisked me into the front room. The musicians were tuning up, the chairs and tables had been lined around the walls and area rugs removed, making a large dance floor.

Father said something to the bandleader and there was an immediate fanfare. People gathered and he waited until as many as could had crowded into the room.

"Friends and neighbors---not only am I celebrating another successful season for Fox Hollow, but this is also a grand night because my daughter is back with us! Now, the first song is for Ellen---I'll start the dancing, then you young bucks can take your turns!"

I groaned inwardly! No one else seemed to find his remark out of the ordinary, however, for there was cheering and applause as the band struck up a spirited version of "Back Home Again In Indiana", and I was whirled around the floor in a fast two-step.

"I wondered where you were, Ellen, I was told you were here but I couldn't find you."

"It's been a strange evening, Father, but you seem to be having a good time!"

"Too bad you aren't---what's the problem?"

"It's quite a story, I'll tell you about it if you'll meet me in your study. I need to borrow a car, too."

His eyebrows lifted. "Sounds interesting, but I can't

meet you too soon, how about in an hour or so. I've got to talk to some people---and so should you---it'd be good for business! You've got the chance to impress some people tonight!

Others were dancing now, and we stopped when someone cut in. It was Rex Post.

"May I, Mr. Jordane?" There was a slight touch of sarcasm, I thought, in the way Rex said 'Mr.', but there was a wide smile on his face and father gladly relinquished his hold on me.

"If it isn't little Foxey-Locksey---all grown up! Yes sir all grown up---welcome back, Ellen!"

I gritted my teeth---if one more person told me how I was 'all grown up'---"Thank you, Rex." I resisted his attempt to pull me close as we danced.

"What's the matter? Are you so happy to see me that you can't stop staring at me?" His pale eyes held a glint of amusement. "I heard you were back in these parts---I've sure missed you! You were the only one that ever got away, and now here you are, back again!"

"Now what does that mean?"

"Forget it---say, aren't you a bit surprised to see me here?"

"No. Rachel told me you'd come. The fact that your parents disapproved of Fox Hollow would not affect your actions. Things have changed since we were kids, Rex, and I have the feeling nothing you'd do would surprise me!"

He laughed. "Good! You sound like just the girl to get outside in the moonlight!"

I knew he was expecting me to object as he led me into the hall and toward the door. "Would you like my jacket around your shoulders, Ellen?"

"No, thanks. We won't be out here long. After all, we can't risk gossip, now can we?"

"Gossip? I never worry about it! Now tell me why you finally decided to come back."

I told him briefly about the shop, I wanted to talk about Rachel, but I was having a hard time bringing her into the conversation without being obvious.

"So, you're here to help Megan---sure that's the only reason? You're not here because you've been pining over some guy you left behind---like me?" His tone was light, but he was standing in the glow of a lantern and his face held no hint that he was teasing.

"You're quite safe, Rex, I won't embarrass you by throwing myself at you---nor do I have designs on anyone else. I didn't even have a date for this evening, I came with Rachel and John."

"John---at the Jordane's---his old man won't like that! He must not have known about it---but I gather John and Rachel have gone---that means he found out where John was and pulled his act!"

"I only know Mrs. Flagg called here asking John to come home, she was very concerned, and, of course, Rachel left with him."

"Bet she was having a fit, too! She's the one that sees thru these stunts the old man pulls. I'm surprised Rachel came tonight, and even more so at John---must have been your influence, you always had a strange effect on him! Ellen, are you sure you didn't come back because of John?"

"Rex! John and I are friends, we always were, you of all people should know that!"

He forced a laugh. "Sure, I know, I was just checking! Just remember that John is not the guy for you Ellen, in fact he's not the guy for any girl! They're all after him, but if one ever does catch him she'll be a sorry girl!"

"Let's go in. It's getting cold!" I was thoroughly angry now.

"Hey, Ellen, don't get me wrong, John and I are still friends, it's just that I know him better than anyone else---I wouldn't say that to anyone but you! John and I always did kind of look out for you---that's what I'm doing now, in a way---"

"You said yourself I was 'all grown up', I'm sure I can look out for myself!"

"Don't be too sure! Things are different around here, even your old man is having to face up to that. You could use a friend, and I can be a very good one!"

"Still the same old Rex---really sold on yourself, aren't you?"

"Don't make me angry, Ellen, you wouldn't want that! Now don't go in all upset---let's make up first!" I had started to walk away, but he grabbed my arm and swung me around to face him. "Foxey-Locksey, I sure missed you---things are going to be a lot more interesting now that you're back! He pulled me to him and kissed me hard---then let me go as suddenly. He walked away, leaving me to stare after him.

It was a moment or two before I realized we had attracted a small audience. I forced myself to walk calmly into the house, going straight to father's study. He wouldn't be there yet, but I wanted to stay hidden until I could borrow a car and get to my motel.

In this room I had received most of my scoldings during my childhood. How I had hated being summoned to the study to face my father! Usually, I had broken the same rules by going to the stables alone, or to the kennels to play with the hounds. There had been times Bertha was in a spiteful mood and would say I had disobeyed just to cause trouble for me. My punishment was confinement to the house with a long list of kitchen duties that I hated. Bertha would be pleased and whistle while she was around me. She had always seemed to be in some kind of contest with me and I was only now starting to understand why.

"Well, Ellen---too much excitement for you?" Father was grinning as he walked in.

"You've already heard---"

"Did you slap Rex's face---no? Moved too fast, did he? You'd better realize you're no longer dealing with those slow-paced Southern gentlemen! Here a man doesn't take forever to let a girl know what's on his mind!"

"I didn't want to make any more of a scene than we already had!"

"Why, no one will think a thing of that! Worse will go on around here before the night's over! Besides, Rex meant it as a compliment---could be he's really interested in you!"

"Now wait---I'll never---"

"Just hold on a minute! I've been thinking about

things this week, you being back could be good for Fox Hollow. Rex has a wild streak in him, all right, but a wife and family has taken that out of many a man! He's been mighty interested in Fox Hollow since his folks died---he's strong as a bull, too. Chances are he could run this place someday!" He rushed my indignation aside, "You just think about it, you may find you don't like running Megan's shop. Then you'd be glad enough to have a husband and family to tend to!"

He was ignoring everything I'd said to him about my work and my plans---everything! Fox Hollow was all that was on his mind. I stood up. I was determined not to argue.

"May I borrow a car? I came with John and Rachel, they were called home shortly after we arrived and I let them take my car. I need a way back to my motel."

"The old Reverend took one of his bad spells again, did he? Probably brought on by John's being here! I'm glad he came, looks good for Fox Hollow. I know he was here because of you---maybe he's a possibility---time was I wouldn't have stood for that, but now he's got a position in the community and he'll be staying, I wouldn't mind at all if you two got together!"

"May I borrow a car or not?"

"No need---just stay here tonight, too early to leave anyway. You should go out there and talk to people, get back in the swing of things!"

"If necessary I'll ask Ersey to loan me his pickup, I'm not staying any longer!"

There was a knock at the door. Father opened it. "Come in---glad you're here, you're right on time!"

I stared, caught completely off guard---it was Mitch.

"Ellen! I hoped I'd see you tonight! Thomas told me you were back. Is this permanent or are you visiting?"

"It's no visit, Mitch, Ellen is playing store, she's here to run Megan's shop---she'll be staying!"

It was just as well father answered for me. I was more affected at seeing Mitch than I could have expected. I searched his eyes. There was nothing but the friendliness of an old acquaintance, glad to see me again---but they were the same brown eyes I'd seen in my dreams, and they warmed me.

"Hello, Mitch. It's very nice to see you. I was just leaving, so I'll go on and let you two have your talk. May I have those keys now?" I turned to face father in time to see a sly expression cross his face.

"Ellen's escort for this evening was John Flagg, but he left her stranded. I'm afraid our local boys have given a bad impression---Rex stole a kiss, to her embarrassment---so now she's ready to call it a night! If it wouldn't be an imposition, perhaps you'd do me the favor of seeing Ellen safely to her motel?"

I was so angry I could barely speak. "Really, Mitch, this is not necessary! I'm taking a car of father's and I can manage for myself. I wouldn't think of taking you away from the party, you just arrived!"

"I'm driving you home. The party will go on for hours. I'll bring my car around front." There was a firmness in his voice that left no room for argument. Mitch left the room and I looked at father. His smugness made my anger flare higher. "How could you maneuver me like that? Do you find it entertaining?"

"Calm down, Ellen! You're not as slick at hiding things as you think---you're interested in Mitch! I thought as much years ago! I wanted to see for myself if you still were, and I got my answer. I've put down some ground work this week with Mitch, I know he has an appreciation of Fox Hollow, and if you let him know how you feel---you'll have it made! That's three good prospects: John, Rex, and Mitch! You've got my blessing---which one you land make me no difference. Surely you can snag one of them."

I jerked the study door open and stomped out. This time I took no pains to disguise my anger and cared nothing for the stir I caused as I stormed out the front door. Mitch met me on the porch steps but I brushed past him and went on to the car.

As he opened the door he said, "Didn't you have a wrap?"

"Oh---I forgot!" I started to get out of the car. He was

smiling, I could tell by his voice when he spoke. "Stay here, just describe it and I'll get it."

I was glad to be alone for a moment as I tried to settle my thoughts. I glanced at the porch and there in the lantern light stood Rex, the look on his face was strange, I couldn't read it. He was staring at the car, at me---surely he knew I could easily see him---I looked away.

When Mitch returned with my wrap I looked again, but Rex was no longer there.

Silently we drove up the hill. At the cedar grove Mitch slowed the car. "Do you mind stopping here, Ellen? I'd like to talk for just a few minutes without dividing my attention with the road."

I moved so I could face him a little more fully. "Mitch, may I please explain about tonight---it's important to me that you know exactly why I'm back. I'm afraid father may have insinuated things that aren't so." I was thinking of father's reference to the "ground work" he had done.

Quickly I brought Mitch up to date, telling him why I was back and the attitude father was taking about my return. I told him why John and Rachel had left the party and explained the way Rex had kissed me. It was easy to talk to Mitch, just as it had been so long ago, and I was feeling much more relaxed. Still, I could only hint at how seriously father was considering him as a possible husband for me.

"I'm sorry you were roped into driving me into town. My father, as I think I once told you, is always the alert matchmaker!"

"Don't worry about it---I know Thomas Jordane rather well. But he's not exactly what I want to talk about. Let's walk, unless you're still in a hurry to leave?"

I smiled at him---the first time I'd done so since he walked into the study, I realized. "A walk would be nice."

As the trees closed in about us, I felt the old enchantment steal over me. The scent of woods and cedar was sharp on the night air. At the opposite edge of the grove we stopped. The moon was well up in the sky now, its light sifting through the branches. Whip-poor-wills were calling across the valley.

Mitch spoke. "Your mood has changed---a few minutes ago you were very angry."

"I was, but not with you."

"You still love it here, don't you?"

"I always will---it's father that makes it impossible for me to stay here---and Bertha!"

"Those two could easily keep anyone off balance. You know, it's hard to explain how it feels to be here with you. We didn't know each other all that well, and it was so long ago---but I never forgot you---"

I held my breath.

"---I asked Bertha for your address. She told me you didn't want her to give it out, that you wanted no reminders of your life here."

"Rachel said Bertha told her much the same, but I'd had no chance to say goodbye to anyone and I wanted to explain so I sent letters to you and Rachel in care of father. I could only trust Bertha would deliver them---I should have known better!"

"None of that matters now---I'm very glad you're back, Ellen, in case I haven't told you."

"Thank you. I'm happy to be back, I just hope father will stop trying to arrange my life! Everything depends on how it goes with the shop---I'm putting it all on the line but I think it will work out." I had my emotions more in hand now, and wanted to steer the conversation to more casual matters. "Why don't you stop by when you've time and see what I'm planning to do with it?"

"I will, and I'd like to show you where I'm working, you'd enjoy Lake Monroe." He went on about his work and I tried to listen, but I was still not believing that I was actually with him---here at Fox Hollow---in the moonlight---

He stopped talking and I realized he was waiting for me to reply! "I'm sorry, Mitch, I was listening---but I just started to get lost in all of this---after all the times I've thought---"

He stepped toward me, bending his head to catch my words. "What did you think?"

I shook my head, I couldn't put into words the way I

felt, not without saying more than was wise.

Without knowing who moved first, he was reaching for me and I was stepping into his arms---now I didn't stop to consider if I was being wise, years of lonely dreaming had convinced me this moment would come and I could only rush to meet it!

Ever so gently he kissed me and then put his face against my hair. Then again his lips were on mine and this time I felt his answering strength as we held each other tightly.

I stood against him and an incredulous flood of happiness rushed through me---now I was really home---only now!

"You're trembling---are you cold?" He drew back to look at me.

I laughed rather shakily. "No, just happy!"

He stepped back. "We'd better go." His voice sounded strangely rough. "I stopped here to talk---I didn't expect this to happen!"

The change in him was so abrupt that I stood unmoving. He must have known my confusion, for he took my arm and started to walk back to the car. He was silent until we had started the drive back toward town.

"Ellen, I know I'm behaving strangely---I admit I wasn't expecting that---I didn't have the slightest intention of kissing you when I stopped back there!"

My thoughts were spinning---why was he suddenly so different---was it something father had said to him---or was there already someone in his life? But my voice was steady and cool as I spoke.

"Mitch, you aren't the first man I've kissed in the moonlight! So, you had a weak moment---a little honest lust is probably good for everyone from time to time!

"Ellen, I'm not like that---"

"No---you're just a good ole boy at heart! It's a tradition you back-home boys like to uphold, right?"

"I don't blame you for being angry---"

"Oh---do I sound angry? I'm sorry! Must be I'm hungry---I'm always grouchy when I'm hungry. John left before we had time for dinner, and I've been rather busy since, so if you'll drop me at the nearest steakhouse I'll appreciate it!" To my utter amazement it was true---I was hungry, so much so that I felt a little lightheaded. I remembered that I had skipped lunch as well.

It was darker in the car than it had been in the moonlight, but I could see Mitch glancing at me when the road allowed it and I was pleased to see that now he looked rather angry himself.

"I told your father I'd see you to your motel, and I will! I was too late for the spread Betha put out, so we'll both eat."

"Suit yourself! But you know what father will think if you're very long in getting back."

"Can't we forget Thomas Jordane for tonight?"

"Forgetting him isn't smart, Mitch, I find he influences almost everything that happens to me---for instance, I'm certain he has said something to you that made you wish you hadn't kissed me tonight!

He made no reply, intent on the twisting road, he was staring straight ahead.

"I can even tell you what it was." I paused, trying to make my voice sound off-hand. "Give poor, love-starved Ellen just a little encouragement and she'll fall into your arms---marry her and all of Fox Hollow is yours, providing she throws off a son or two to keep it going!" We were coming into town now and I could see him plainly. "Am I close?"

He nodded. "Close."

"Well, don't panic, Mitch---he probably said the same things to Rex, thinking some competition would help things along! At least he hasn't talked to John---yet! But father thinks Fox Hollow is a prize any man would want, even if he had to marry me to get it!"

"You and Fox Hollow make quite a package, Ellen, don't kid yourself about that."

"What am I going to do? I've been in town one week and he's trying to marry me off!"

"Let's have a good meal and forget it all for tonight."

I had not even noticed he had stopped the car. "Fine!

I'm too angry to talk about it anymore."

Inside we were shown to a secluded table. A waitress moved quickly toward us.

"Hello Penny."

"Hi Mitch. Are you ready to order?" She looked us over, taking in every detail of my gown. "Where's Denise--- out of town?"

Mitch nodded and she flounced away, making it plain to us both that she did not approve of us.

"You're sure just plain salad, steak and baked potato is all you want, Ellen?"

"I trust your choice, you apparently eat here often! I'm sure I'm supposed to ask who Denise is!"

Mitch grinned. "Penny wasn't exactly subtle. Denise and I come here so often Penny assumes we're a steady twosome."

"A steady twosome---how endearingly solid and old fashioned that sounds! Certainly much safer than allowing yourself to be swept off your feet!"

He met my eyes, "I'll just have to stay out of the moonlight." His voice was low, with some of the roughness I'd heard when he kissed me.

The waitress returned at that moment and briskly set our plates in front of us.

"It's all right, Penny, Mitch and I knew each other when we were much younger, that's all."

"That's nice." She spoke without a smile and walked away.

"Now, Mitch, tell me about Rex. Rachel is going to be hurt by him, I'm afraid. And I want to know what he does for a living."

"I don't think Rex takes Rachel seriously. He has someone running the store his parents had, a country grocery is too small an operation to interest him. He wheels and deals in a little of everything, he knows people from one end of the state to the other."

We were eating nearly as fast as we were talking. The food was delicious and it was making me more steady, for that I was indeed grateful. Mitch went on.

"I had a horse your father let me board at Fox Hollow and I rode there often. When I wanted to sell it, Rex took it off my hands. He buys horses from others around, he always knows someone in the market for one. Of course, he makes a little on the deal, plus he's bought and sold some land here and there---he's got his hand in several things."

"I see. You said you know father rather well---how did that come about? I know you never cared for fox hunting."

"I knew some of the people who worked for him, I even worked for him myself the summer after my freshman year---before I transferred to the university at Carbondale, Illinois. I groomed horses, painted, mowed, all sorts of things."

"I didn't know that." I found it strange to think of Mitch being at Fox hollow while I was away, missing it so.

"After college I worked out of state awhile. But when I came back and started working in the Lake Monroe project, your father asked me to come see him." He signaled for another pot of coffee. Penny brought it with even less enthusiasm than the first.

"I think we're lingering too long; Penny is not happy with us!"

"Penny isn't going to get a tip either, if she keeps it up!"

Somehow, I was glad to see Mitch annoyed with the waitress---perhaps because I felt she was the unknown Denise's defender!

"What did father want to see you about?"

"He was worried about the sudden shortage of foxes; this was two seasons ago. There were two reasons, aside from the fact they had been hunted so many years---Thomas was being too thorough about cleaning up has land, he wasn't leaving enough natural cover, and like most animals foxes have cycles of scarcity and abundance. That was a year of severe scarcity for the fox."

"Did that explanation satisfy father?"

"It had to---he didn't want to talk to anyone else about it and risk rumors. He even had to bring in a fox for one of his more important hunts."

"A bag fox! That would hurt his reputation! Bringing in a fox and turning it loose to hunt is considered one of the most unsporting things one can do! I gather this past season found things more normal?"

He nodded. "There have been no more bag foxes." He was watching me intently. I had the feeling he wanted to ask about my life with Megan and suddenly I didn't want to reveal anymore about myself. So, I said the first thing I could think of.

"What does your work involve? I'm sure you told me earlier, but I missed it." In spite of myself I felt my face turn pink.

He grinned. "I have a B.S. in conservation, some background in soils and geology, tech drawing and elementary surveying. I'm working now more in park and wildlife management. I'm happy with what I do."

"I'm glad." Mitch had answered a lot of questions, but I was as unsure of things as before.

We left the restaurant and, in the car, I told him the name of my motel. The ride was short and for me, rather strained. We didn't speak until we were at my door.

"I hope the party isn't too far gone by the time you're back."

"I'm not in the mood for a party after all---your father will have to think whatever he pleases!"

I shrugged, "He will! Good night, Mitch."

"Good night, Ellen---be careful!"

I was inside the room and had the lights on before I heard him drive away.

So, now I knew---Mitch had not been waiting for me! I stood leaning against the door. Now that I was alone the emotions I'd held at arm's length flooded over me---I'd gone from anticipation to anger, from hopefulness to despair, and there was no one with whom I could share any of it! Megan, I knew, would tell me prayer was the answer at a time like this---but the old Reverend Flagg had always said it was a waste of time for women to pray, that God had little patience with them after Eve led Adam astray---and those words still seemed to get in my way.

Later, as I was trying to fall asleep, all the jumbled impressions of the evening faded away at the thought of those few minutes beneath the tall cedars with Mitch. For that brief time everything had been right. Could it ever happen again? I only knew if it did, I would try with all my being to make him forget Denise!

When sleep finally came, it was troubled by dreams of Mitch calling to me from somewhere at Fox Hollow, and although I tried to find him, at each turn I saw only Rex whose laughter at my frantic search was hauntingly evil. John quietly watched from a distance, unable to help me and looking incredibly sad at my plight.

When morning plucked me out of my nightmare, my face was wet with tears. The dawn held little reassurance and I couldn't lose the feeling that my dream had been a prediction of things to come.

Five

After I'd showered and dressed, I opened the drapes to bright sunshine. If I were with Megan, we'd be on our way to church---I was just realizing there were several things I'd miss sharing with her.

"Ellen! Are you awake?" It was Rachel, banging loudly on my door.

"Come in---I was just thinking of going out for breakfast, come with me!"

"Not in this! To think I borrowed this dress from mom so I wouldn't feel silly driving through town in the gown I wore to the party last night!"

I had to grin, the print housedress was too long and much too tight for Rachel's shapely form. Her hair was still in the elegant upsweep, although it looked ready to tumble down at any moment.

"As Bertha would say, you look like two pounds of bologna in a one-pound sack!"

"Well! Thanks! John talked me into staying the night at the folks'. None of us got much sleep and I can't wait to get back to my own apartment! How about if I fix breakfast for both of us?"

I grabbed my purse and locked the door behind us. "How is your father---I take it he's improved?"

"John and I both thank you for the loan of your car last night. As for dad, well---I don't think I can go through this act of his one more time! You should see it---that's the only way you'd believe it!"

"You mean he really was pretending---just to get John away from the party?"

"Oh yes---mom let it slip that John had gone. So, we called the doctor and went through all the motions, but John is the only one who really swallows it---I'm sure mom sees through it, though she doesn't say so. John seems to almost worship dad and I can't see why---he's never gotten one word of praise from him! Dad demands more from him all the time and John does his absolute best to deliver!"

"What more can he possibly ask of John?"

"Oh---get church attendance up---never mind that it's better than it ever was when day was preaching---bigger offerings, dad wants a new church built---but on top of the list, get married and have a son to carry on as pastor of the church someday! My grandfather built that church and dad thinks the world would end if there wasn't a Flagg in the pulpit!"

"He puts that much pressure on John?"

"All the time! I don't know how John takes it, but he never even gets angry with dad over it."

I pulled in at the curb. "I'm really ready for that coffee, I didn't sleep very well last night either."

But Rachel was already out of the car. "Hurry up Ellen, I don't want to be seen in this dress!"

Inside I glanced about the small living room. The walls and carpet were beige, it was furnished sparingly but comfortably with a pale green and beige striped sofa and two chairs, one in a matching stripe and the other in the solid green. The end tables were wicker, which added to the feeling of airiness Rachel had achieved. A Boston fern spilled over its stand and English ivy in hanging planters brightened one wall. Behind them hunt a rattan floor mat, giving texture and interest to the area.

"Rachel, I really like the way you've done this---I would never have thought of putting that mat on the wall."

While I had been looking around, she had changed into a robe and busied herself in the kitchen.

"Surprised?"

"No, of course not---just impressed! Partly with myself for having the smarts to ask you to work at the shop---you'll be a wizard at doing the window!"

"You'd let me do the displays? I'd love that! Toast and eggs okay? That's about all I can cook."

"Sounds good. Rachel, if you don't mind my asking, just how does your father go about pretending these attacks?"

"Well, first he gets mom all upset, then demands she call John and me---he does a lot of gasping and clutching at his chest. Then he starts in on how he has prayed to live long enough to see John marry---but it just isn't to be---his time has come---" Rachel was mocking her father's voice, rolling her eyes and gesturing the same way I remembered her doing years ago when she had a story to tell!

"---by this time John has called the doctor, then dad starts on how he's lived a near perfect life and is longing to go to is reward---how we'll all see a true Christian die, without fear---he just goes on like that until the doctor comes and tells him he's alright!"

"How hard this must be for your mother---for all of you!"

"Well, he'll cry 'wolf' one time too many if he isn't careful. Now, let's eat---and I want to hear about last night, just start with what happened after John and I left, tell me all about it!"

I dropped my eyes from her gaze and busied myself buttering toast. What would she say if she knew Rex had kissed me?

"The first thing father did was announce to everyone I

was back. I was so embarrassed when he said, 'I'll start the dancing, then you young bucks can take your turns!' Young bucks! Of all the things to say in public!"

Rachel was grinning. "So, who did you dance with?"

"Rex cut in right away. We didn't dance long, he was intent on charming me, and I know he thought he was quite successful!" I took a swallow of coffee and plunged on "We went out on the porch to talk and he kissed me---nothing personal about it, just a quick buzz to show me he could get away with it---but it made me angry, several people saw us."

"I know about that."

"You know---how?"

"Bertha called at the crack of dawn on the pretext of asking about dad, but she went on about the party and what a success it was---managing, of course, to tell me Rex had kissed you, which was her sole purpose in calling in the first place! But I'm glad you told me---it's nice to hear you say it meant nothing!" She shrugged and flashed a quick smile. "That's Rex's way."

"Rachel! How can you not be angry? You said you love him."

"I do. But Rex is always looking for the best deal, he'll want to see if you'll give him a chance. I'm used to this, I've waited out more girls than I care to count!"

"I'm glad you aren't angry at me---I don't want anything to spoil our friendship. I know that was what Bertha was hoping to do. She doesn't want me to make a go of the shop, she want me back in North Carolina with Megan! I think she has some plan and she feels I'm a threat---as for Rex, I'll make certain he knows where he stand with me ---if he doesn't already!"

"I knew you would, Ellen, I'm not really worried. But say, didn't you think John looked handsome last night?"

"Yes, he did, he's very good looking! But half the female population of Greene County is going to be gunning for me---they were barely civil when John introduced me. Doesn't he have an interest in anyone? Some of those girls were really quite attractive. I'm sure your father would approve of at least one of them!"

"Oh, he would! He's so anxious for John to marry he's past being choosey!"

"He must be---you did say he'd even approve of me!"

She laughed, "Come on now! But it's true, he'd be pleased if you two married, and so would I!"

"John and I have too nice a friendship---marriage would spoil it!"

"Why do you say that?" Her voice was sharp, the teasing smile was gone.

"No reason---I'm only joking---", but I remembered Rex's odd remark that the girl who married John would be sorry--- "what's wrong, Rachel, what's this all about?"

Her eyes met mine and I could see the struggle in their dark depths. I spoke softly, "I don't mean to pry, you needn't tell me. But I can see something is bothering you, and if you want to talk about it---you know I'll listen."

"Oh, Ellen---could I tell you---would you understand and not think any less of John?" She reached across the little table and grasped my hand as if she were trying to draw something from me. "Just promise me that you won't change toward John!"

"You know I value John's friendship---I can't imagine anything causing me to think badly of him."

"John does not have the ability---or even the desire--- to love any woman---not physically!"

I sat still, staring at her. Was this what Rex had hinted at---could he know this about John?

"John and I are two misfits from a mis-matched marriage---and neither of us can change!"

"If John could get professional help---"

"Oh, Ellen, he's been through that---when he was away school. He didn't confide in me until he'd done all he could to understand himself! The thing is, he's accepted it--- in fact he seems not to mind at all! If it weren't for dad's insistence that he marry, John would probably be comfortable with his---his lot---but he feels as if he's letting dad down and he can't stand that!"

"Would your father possibly be able to understand, if John explained---"

"No! He would never understand or accept John if he knew---he'd say it was the devil living in John---just what he says about me---it would just kill John!"

"Does your mother know?"

"She wonders why John shows no interest in seeing anyone, but she finds excuses---she probably thinks he takes after dad when it comes to the physical aspect of love---a very low level of interest! Mom would feel better if John married, if only to shut dad up. But I'm certain she has no idea of the real reason."

"What is the reason---did he tell you?

"There's a lot to it, but it boils down to two things, and you can take your choice as to what you believe. Personally, I think John was so affected by the way dad constantly belittled women that he grew up not knowing how to react! In dad's sermons, at home in the way he treated mom and me---it was a constant campaign to prove men are far above women in the eyes of God! A man marries when the time comes, he has sons---that's his duty, and once fulfilled, well, then he has a housekeeper for whom he has only to provide room and board! I know that's the way he looks at life. And he expects John to see it the same way. I guess I'm hoping the right woman will break through the mental blocks dad created in John!"

"I remember how your father was! Is this the theory John accepts?"

"He tries very hard not to! As John points out, it says in the Bible some men will be born as eunuchs---John says he can be more single minded in doing his work. I think that's why he accepts this without any bitterness. But I guess what you've never known or wanted, you never miss!"

"Then Rachel, why have you tried to push us together ever since I've been back?"

"I pushed so many girls at him he had to tell me the truth to stop me. But it's different with you, he doesn't mind---and maybe I hoped you'd be the right one for him. You've always been a special friend to him---now that I've told you this, are you still?"

"I'm touched that you trust me enough to tell me. If

anything, I'll feel more comfortable with John than before. Usually, I feel like a prize heifer up for bids, in fact, father has let it be known that that's how it is! But I feel John likes me simply as a person, nothing more, and that's a relief!"

"Thank you, Ellen, I won't ever be sorry I told you."

"John and I have a lot in common, our fathers are both pressuring us for marriage and grandsons! John just feels a greater guilt at not granting that wish. At this point I'm no more likely to marry than John!"

"Now why would you say that?"

"As soon as I came back, father started making plans for me. He told Rex and even Mitch Kramer that I'm up for grabs, whoever gets me gets Fox Hollow! I can hardly trust the motives of any man I know now, except John."

Rachel was regarding me with a thoughtful, almost secretive look. "I know how you feel about Rex, but what about Mitch, he must have been at the party?"

"I like him, and he is very nice and considerate---" I couldn't tell her the truth and I thought she knew I was holding back "---what I think of him doesn't matter anyway, he's all but engaged to someone named Denise. They have an understanding; I believe was the way he put it!"

"Oh, yes, Denise! I didn't know they were that serious!"

"You know her? What's she like?" I got up and refilled our coffee cups, mostly to give myself time to hide the jealous curiosity behind my questions.

"I don't really know her; I saw her around campus. Her family is high society in Philadelphia. Denise is here finishing up her masters degree in theater or dance---or some such---I've seen her with Mitch---it'll never work! He's just a change from the men she's used to. She's temporarily fascinated with the rugged, outdoor type. She'll never settle for Mitch!"

"Mitch must be just as fascinated with her."

"Well, it would be understandable---she's classy looking! She has unusual eyes, sort of violet, and long, blond hair---natural---dresses like a million bucks---she sure knows how to charm the men!"

"Okay, I've got the picture! She wouldn't be one of those girls you waited for Rex to tire of, would she?"

"Oh, Rex didn't tire of Denise---she wouldn't even give him the time of day! He still can't believe it!" Rachel laughed, but I heard the bitterness in her voice.

I thought of the waitress at the restaurant last night, she was certainly one of Denise's admirers. But Rachel was not, nor would I be---and for the same reason---we were jealous! And I, at least, had considerable cause!

"Rachel, I'm going to the shop and try to get some book work done. Maybe this week you can go apartment hunting with me?"

"Sure, anytime. And thanks, Ellen, for understanding about John. I feel so much better about everything!"

Again, I caught something secretive in Rachel's smile as she closed the door behind me. In the car I thought over what she'd told me about John. Why had I not been shocked---certainly, Rachel had expected me to be. But I could sympathize with John, the reasons were different but still his situation was somewhat like my own.

I'd had no real interest in any man I'd ever met, other than Mitch Kramer, and now I was certain he was beyond my reach. I was no match for the dazzling Denise! It had not really been me Mitch had kissed under the cedars---it had been a memory he was fond of, and at that, it had been a kiss of goodbye. The realization hurt. How unfair that two people could share one kiss and feel such different emotions. How foolish of me to have assumed his were the same as my own!

Inside the shop I locked the door behind me. There was a seldom used mail slot in the door and something light colored in the basket caught my eye---usually mail was too bulky for the slot and, besides, I'd been here when the mail came yesterday. I took the small envelope out of the basket and walked back to the office. I sat down at the desk, feeling an uneasy stir as I drew out the slip of paper.

"Foxey-Locksey, go home to Megan. Don't wait. You know what happens to a fox in a trap."

I held the paper and stared at it until the neatly

printed letters blurred---I knew very well what happened to the fox! If a dog didn't find it and kill it in a vicious and predictable battle, it either chewed its foot off to escape or it was shot by the trapper while it was held as a perfect target!

Was I being stalked---was someone waiting to catch me in a trap? But there was no reason! It could only be Bertha, taking a sadistic pleasure in frightening me.

I'd drive to Fox Hollow right now and tell her I had no intention of leaving---or of putting up with her tricks! If she didn't stop, I'd tell father what she was doing, that would settle it!

I put the note in my pocket and gathered up the bookkeeping records. As I unlocked the front door it was suddenly pushed open. I could only step backward to keep from being knocked off balance.

"Lucky I got here when I did or I'd have missed you! Rachel told me you'd be here doing some book work."

"Rex Post---what do you mean by forcing your way in here---what do you want?"

"Say, Ellen, I didn't mean to scare you! Guess you couldn't have seen me through that door blind---I thought you were unlocking the door to let me in! I'd knocked once, you must not have heard---I'm sorry, kid!" He put his arm around my shoulders and steered me to a chair.

"Sit down and catch your breath. Now, I stopped by to apologize---I hear you're pretty mad at me for kissing you in front of those people last night! Guess I should have known better, just wasn't thinking! You looked good and I just did what came naturally. Am I forgiven?" He stood grinning down at me.

I stared up at him, trying to decide if he was telling the truth.

"I'd have told you this last night, but you took off. I am sorry you didn't feel you could ask me to drive you home, I'd have been happy to do it! I did notice old Mitch never made it back to the party---wonder what happened?" He was still grinning, but there was a cool glint in his eyes.

"Mitch drove me home because father gave him no choice---John and Rachel had my car and I wanted to leave--

-when I asked to borrow a car, father insisted Mitch drive me, that's all there was to it! If Mitch decided not to come back to the party, that's something you'll have to ask him about, if you're really that interested!"

"Maybe Mitch decided to spend the rest of the evening with Denise---you know about Denise, I guess?" Rex was watching me intently.

"Yes, I do. Mitch told me about her."

"No kidding! Mitch told you! Now that is rude---a guy talking about another girl when he's with you---Mitch is the one who should be apologizing!"

"Look, Rex, I know what father told you and Mitch about me---I find it embarrassing and insulting! You can stop all this pretense of a sudden interest in me---it'll get you nowhere! You don't care for me---Mitch is in love with Denise---so you're both out of the running! It will be up to me to find myself a husband, all by myself, if I ever decide I want one! So let's forget all this silliness!"

"So you think I'm being silly? I didn't intend to give you that impression! I'd better set the record straight right now!"

He took the books from my lap and put them on the table beside my chair. Taking both my hands, he pulled me to my feet.

"Rex, if you think---"

"Now be still, Ellen, and listen to what I'm going to say, I want no misunderstanding about this!" He slid his hands up to my elbows, pinning my arms to my sides. "Your old man has the same as given me the go-ahead to marry you if I can get the job done---and I like the idea, I like it fine! You can act as uppity as you want, but we both know Thomas Jordane has a way of getting what he wants. This time I'm happy to help him get it! I'd be great at running Fox Hollow---you ought to hear my plans---"

"Let go of me---and get out of here or I'll---"

"What? Scream if you want to---no one will hear you!"

I stared at him---he was right, no one would hear me, and I was afraid to risk making him angrier.

"As I was saying, I've got big plans for Fox Hollow, and you could do a lot worse than me! I know you didn't like my kissing you in public, but we're alone now, and I don't think you'll mind at all this time!"

I tried to turn away, but he put his mouth hard on mine. He was still holding my arms against my sides and now he pressed them tightly in against my ribs---forcing the very breath from me. He held me that way for an endless time, then whispered in my ear, his voice cold and determined.

"This is how it's going to be, Ellen, so get used to the idea!" He moved toward the door, then stopped. "I decided a long time ago you were the one I really wanted. I thought you'd got away from me, but now you're back---guess it was meant to be all along!"

It was long after Rex left before I took the books and went out to my car. I had just stood---wondering what to do. I'd told Rex he had no chance with me, just as I'd told Rachel I would do, but he had not listened.

My father has as much as told Rex he can marry me! My father! As always, he was the cause of my troubles! Finally, I started the car and drove toward Fox Hollow. Talking to Bertha could wait, it was father I wanted to talk to now---and I would force him to listen. My mind was spinning with all I intended to say, and I tried to force my thoughts into order as I drove.

There were no other cars about when I stopped in front of the house. Everything was still, the lanterns hanging on the porch were the only reminders of last night's festivities. I knocked loudly. I was about to go in when Bertha opened the door, looking as cross and put out as she sounded.

"Don't have to tear the door down---ought to know I'd be restin', what in the world do you want?"

"To talk to father, where is he?"

"At the stables, far as I know, but he'll be comin' to the house soon 'cause he told---asked---me to make a pot of coffee. It's waitin' now. Might as well come on in."

I shook my head and hurried down the walk. Quiet,

sun-filled afternoons like this one had soothed my bad
moods many times in the past, this time my anger was
beyond its reach. As I stormed up to the stables, I met father
coming out.

"Well, Ellen, I didn't expect to see you back today.
Since you're here, come see this new mare---just bought her
last week!"

"Another time. I want to talk to you."

I could sense the air of amusement that he had always
maintained when he knew I was angry. He stepped out of
the dimness of the stables and now I could see the slight
smile turn the corners of his mouth.

"What's on your mind?"

Ersey Hunter appeared behind father. "Why, if it ain't
little Ellen! Glad you're back---and ain't you all growed up!"
He was grinning at me, plainly happy to see me. Now, the
sight of a genuinely friendly face was a balm to my raw
nerves, and I hugged Ersey, an act out of character for a
Jordane.

"It's great to see you, Ersey---I missed you!"

"Missed you too, child---sure did!" He patted my
shoulder and with a pleased but embarrassed look on his
sun-wrinkled face, he went past us on toward the house.

"So, you missed old Ersey---I'm glad to know you
missed someone!"

I turned back to face my father. There was no hint of
a smile on his face now. "Are we alone?"

"Quite. You know I don't keep anyone here on Sunday
when we're not hunting. I still run Fox Hollow much as
always."

"Oh yes! I know how you enjoy running things---my
life for example!"

"Ellen, you've been upset about one thing or another
ever since you came back---you'd better get a grip on
yourself. You can't run a business if you're so
temperamental all the time. Now let's go to the house and
have a bite to eat, we'll talk in the study."

As usual, he had managed to gain control of the
situation and I followed along behind him. It still was hard

not to let him get the upper hand. But not this time, I promised myself, I would say what I had come to say!

Father opened the kitchen door for me and Bertha turned to look at us. "Didn't know you was stayin' to eat. I'll put another place on."

"Just bring a tray to the study, Bertha---Ellen and I have something to discuss." He spoke as he washed his hands at the kitchen sink.

"I'll just have coffee, Bertha." She raised an eyebrow at me in a way that said I was lucky to get even that from her. I remembered the note in my pocket---if I had the chance I'd tell her I knew she was behind it, but it was no longer the most important reason I was here.

While I was anxious to plunge into the reason I'd come, I didn't want to be interrupted when Bertha brough the tray, so I said the first thig I could think of.

"The house looked lovely for the party; it was all very impressive."

"I'm glad you thought so. You were in such a lather to leave last night I didn't think you'd notice!"

He was trying to goad me, I knew. "Oh, I noticed. I understand you have your parties catered now."

He made no reply but studied me with a steady gaze. I wondered what he was thinking.

A tap signaled Bertha's arrival and father opened the door. Scowling, she put a full tray on the desk and left, slamming the door just enough to make her displeasure clear. It brought only a chuckle from father.

"All right Ellen, we can get down to brass tacks--- what's the problem today?" His tone managed to make it sound as if I made a habit of running to him with petty problems.

"I've talked to Mitch, and to Rex, and I know what you told them about me! I resent it---more than I can say!"

"I noticed Mitch never made it back to the party--- what happened?" He was half smiling again, turning the subject to suit himself.

"Mitch took me home, where he went afterward is none of my business or yours. I know for a fact he's interested in someone named Denise!"

"Oh---that won't last, she's all wrong for Mitch---I've been told she's a big-city girl, she'd never last here, too dull for her!"

"I only came to talk about Rex Post! I know you the same as told him he can marry me---now you can tell him to leave me alone!"

"He can marry you as far as I'm concerned---why should I tell him anything else?"

"Rex thinks you practically gave him permission to--- to---" I faltered, searching for an acceptable way to word what I could not bring myself to say. "---Rex was in the shop today, he kissed me and---"

"Is this what all this hysteria is about---so Rex kissed you again! What's wrong with you, Ellen? Didn't Megan tell you anything of what to expect from men---didn't she tell you how to handle incidents like this? Seems to me that's a mother's duty to her daughter. Surely Rex isn't the first man to make a serious pass at you---or is he?"

"What did you say---" My mind stopped for a moment, I couldn't have heard correctly!

"I asked if Rex is the first man to make a pass at you!"

"No---before that---you asked if my mother---"

"Ellen, I've got no more patience for these imagined threats to your virginity! It's no more than any other girl has to put up with---if Megan didn't teach you how to handle such things, don't come crying to me---it's not my problem! You can't learn to swim if you don't get in the water!"

Suddenly, his words seemed to swell inside my head until I thought it would burst! I could hear my pulse pounding in my ears. The floor seemed to tilt, and I grabbed the arms of the chair, I shut my eyes against the sickening sway of the walls. From what seemed a great distance I could hear my own voice--- "My mother is dead---Claudette is dead---"

"Ellen, Megan is your mother---didn't she tell you? You spent all those years with her---I was sure you knew!"

Rage threatened to engulf me, and I managed a feeble attempt to control it. "I lived fifteen years here with you---

why didn't you tell me the truth?"

"There were reasons---yes, there were---don't shake your head! You don't know anything about it!"

"How can I be sure you are even my father? Megan was married to your brother, maybe Uncle Charles was my father!"

"I'm your father, Ellen, I can prove it if you want." He spoke tiredly, "I always thought Megan wanted to take you to North Carolina just to keep you away from Fox Hollow---to get even with me---I wouldn't have blamed her! She knew after Nolan died I needed to keep you here so you'd raise your children at Fox Hollow and I'd have my grandsons to leave all this to. I thought she was trying to hurt me through you!

I stood up carefully, but my head was clear now, painfully so. "I don't know if I believe this, why wasn't I told long ago---why let me think Claudette was my mother---she never loved me, I always knew she didn't!"

"That's not wholly true, Ellen---Claudette was very good to you, even more so after she had Nolan! Then she no longer had any reason to be jealous of you---we had our own child."

"Oh, yes, I remember how it was---" Now my voice was shaking, raging out of my control, prodded by the years of hurt I'd never understood. "---when Nolan was alive, I was part of the family, but from the day he died I was excluded from everything! I just ate and slept in this house! I loved Nolan too---I missed him---but you turned away from me---you never touched me, you didn't talk to me---it was as if I'd done some dreadful thing and no one would tell me what it was!"

"And how else could you expect me to react---I think I treated you a great deal better than most men would under the circumstances! I didn't touch you because I was afraid if I did I'd beat you to an inch of your life! Had you been older I well might have---but you were only nine---too young, perhaps, to have been entrusted with his care."

"But why were you angry at me because Nolan fell down the stairs---I wasn't with him, I was outside---"

73

"Yes, I know! Bertha showed me the wildflowers you'd slipped off to pick when you'd been told to watch Nolan!"

"No! That's not how it was---I always took good care of him when I was told to watch him---I loved him---I found him, I was the one who reached him first!"

"Yes, you found him---you knew you'd left him unattended too long and you ran back inside and found my son---dead! Bertha told me how it was, and Claudette agreed with her account---you didn't watch Nolan as you'd been told and as a result, he fell! His death broke our hearts--- Claudette had ignored her doctor's advice by having Nolan, it was definite she would never have another child. Claudette was not a strong woman in any sense of the word, and she began to drink heavily---Nolan's death ruined her life!"

He stood looking out the window as if remembering it all made it impossible for him to look at me.

"Father, turn around, look at me!" He turned slowly. Framed by the sun-filled window his face was cold and bleak. "All this time I've never known that you and mother--- Claudette---believed I was responsible---I wondered countless times why you both seemed to hate me! But it isn't true---I was not told to watch Nolan or I would have done it! Bertha has lied about this, either she or Claudette must have let him out of their sight---but it was not me---please--- believe me!"

With no change of expression, he walked past me and out of the room. I felt for the chair behind me and sank into it. *He thinks it was my fault Nolan died!*

It was too much for me to comprehend and I sat, unmoving.

"You still here? I seen Mr. Jordane goin' down to the stables so I came for the tray---now what's wrong with him---this food ain't been touched or the coffee neither!" She gathered things onto the tray as she talked.

"Bertha, why did you lie to father the day Nolan died?"

"What? What crazy thing you sayin'?"

"I know you told him it was my fault Nolan fell, he

told me so just now. You know it's a lie---was it your fault?"

"Listen here, Missy, you came back here strictly uninvited and you'd been better off to stay where you was! Now I'm gonna give you some good advice it ain't too late to take!" She went to the door and closed it. Looming over my chair she leaned toward me and spoke in a low voice. "Now, I done make my plans, ain't no way you can change 'em! You just stay in town, tend to that dress store and leave us at Fox Hollow alone---then you'll be all right! I ain't told nothin' about Nolan's dyin' that ain't so---don't try to say I did just to save face at this late date!"

The look in Bertha's black eyes was enough to keep me in my chair had I had the strength to stand, which I doubted. I was at her mercy and she knew it as well as I.

"If you get stubborn about this, you'll be sorry. All you Jordane women been stubborn---Claudette was---she'd be alive today if she'd give up and left your father like I told her she should when she finally believed he'd been after her money all along! And Megan---she could have all this if she'd just say the word, but no---she's too stubborn just 'cause Thomas jilted her once! Good thing she's like that, never can tell what might happen to her here at Fox Hollow! And it's hard to say what might happen to you if you go stirrin' things up!"

"So---it was you who called me that night, and the note today---"

"I don't know nothin' about none of that---why would I go to all that trouble when I can tell you face to face what I think of you bein' here? Sounds like you got enemies you don't even know!" She chuckled. "Poor little Ellen---time was you'd run off to the woods with your troubles---but you got no place to run now! Your father don't want no part of you---you got no mother, not that wants you---"

"You know---"

"Sure I know! I knowed years ago! Ain't you never wondered why your middle name is Paige? It was Megan that gave you that, sure wasn't Claudette's idea! I know why Megan Paige Jordane was here that last time---Claudette was drinkin' that day she decided to ride in the hunt, and she told me what the two of them had cooked up! Megan was to come and get you---Megan wanted you and Claudette was finally ready for her to take you, she couldn't stand the sight of you no more!"

"Why? Why was Claudette finally willing for me to leave?" I was sure of the answer, yet I needed to hear Bertha place the blame on me for myself before I could believe she would do it!

"'cause you was Megan's---but mostly 'cause she couldn't look at you without thinkin' of her baby boy---you cost her her only hold on her husband! She couldn't forgive you that! So, she drank to forget---then with a word from me here and there, she came up with a plan. And it was a good one, but Claudette messed it up when she decided to ride in the hunt---I tried to talk her out of it, but she was afraid of Thomas. She thought if she was away from the house when Megan took you, he wouldn't find out she was plottin' against him. Her thinkin' was clouded by drinkin' too much that mornin'---"

"Bertha, you in there?" It was Ersey.

"I think we got us a understandin' now, Miss Jordane!" She stepped back and winked at me. "I'm comin', Ersey." She opened the door wide. "Gotta get this tray. Me and Ellen was just jawin' a bit."

She sailed off down the hall and with a questioning glance at me, Ersey followed.

Was I wrong---had it been as they said---had I neglected Nolan?

It was so long ago, had I tried to protect myself by turning around what I could not accept as fact? A child's mind might easily do that over a period of time.

Woodenly, I picked up my purse and went outside. No one was in sight as I started the car and drove up the hill My hands started to shake so I pulled off the drive and got out of the car. The soft breeze ruffling the cedars reached out to stroke my hot face.

Bertha was right about one thing---I'd made a big mistake in coming back to Fox Hollow! Today the old trees remembered me, and they seemed to agree, for I could hear them whisper---silly Ellen---silly Ellen---

Six

When I finally looked out my window the sun was already hiding behind the town. All afternoon I had mulled over everything father and Bertha had said. Still, nothing they told me about Nolan's death coincided with my own memories of that day.

How I longed to talk to someone! There was only John, he was the only one I could count on to understand. Rachel had said Reverend Flagg was all right---John might have time to see me---I was dialing even as I thought. I was relieved when John answered.

"John, it's Ellen. Are you busy? I'm sorry to bother you but Rachel said your father was better and---"

"Wait, Ellen, don't talk so fast! What is it, have you had another of those phone calls?"

"No," I steadied myself, just hearing a calm voice was helping. "If everything is all right at home, could you possible see me this evening---I can be there right after your evening service."

"It's over promptly at eight, but I'll come there, where are you staying?"

Gratefully, I gave him the address. Now to pass the time until he arrived---a walk would help. The motel was only a few blocks from the downtown area, I'd go window shopping.

I grabbed a sweater. Traffic was light and there seemed to be an unhurried air about the few people strolling along the sidewalks. There was something different about a town on Sunday evenings. I liked the slower pace. If only my thoughts would stop rushing back and forth!

I studied the windows of Alyson's, then Wick's, but soon I forgot the windows and was walking rapidly. After a few blocks I was in the campus area.

Once Megan had walked along these same streets, and Uncle Charles---why had father not attended the university---I realized I knew little about his earlier life. Only that he had grown up in Virginia, and it was there he had learned to love horses and fox hunting.

It struck me how little I really knew about any of the people who were the most important in my life. I sat down on the low stone wall running along the sidewalk. I had been such a solitary, unquestioning child, and I'd changed little in that respect as I grew older---until now!

Surely there had been signs---if I'd given any indication of having seen them, Megan would have told me the truth---wouldn't she?

I started back to the motel, walking slower now, tired of my silent tug-of-war. I chose a different route back, intending to stop for a cup of coffee. I turned a corner. In front of a theater, a line of people were buying tickets for the nine o'clock movie. I checked my watch, it was nearly eight thirty, I'd have to skip the coffee. I still had several blocks to walk.

I glanced at the people, feeling a twinge of envy for the pleasant evening they were enjoying. I stopped. It was Mitch, standing with his back to me. And there could be no mistake about the laughing girl facing him---it had to be

Denise! She looked to be all Rachel had said---so much for the small hope that Rachel had exaggerated this morning! I turned quickly and went on. I knew Mitch had not seen me; Denise held his attention far too firmly.

Back in my motel room, I turned on all the lights, went to the mirror, brushed my hair and retouched my make-up. Father and Rachel had both said it would not last between Mitch and Denise. Now that I'd seen her, I was sure they were wrong.

"Ellen---let me in---my hands are full!"

"I'm coming!" I unlocked the door. "What do you have here---I smell coffee!"

"You do. I stopped for some just down the street to go with all this sandwich material I brought from home. The ladies of the church are so good about helping out when father has one of these bad times. There's always more than we can use."

I watched in surprise as he spread things out on the only table the room offered.

"I remembered your fondness for pickles, so I brought some of those big dills mother puts up."

"How did you know I hadn't eaten? And pickles---"

"Well Ellen! Don't cry! They're just plain old pickles, not as special as all that!"

I had to laugh, even as I blinked against the moisture threatening to spill against my will. "I know---this is just so kind of you! I can't believe you remembered about the pickles! I was just dying for some coffee, too!"

"I would have bet my hymn book you hadn't eaten, you're even thinner than when you first came back! And besides, I'm hungry, so let's eat and talk later."

We scooted the two chairs closer to the table. It was a slightly inconvenient arrangement, but his obvious enjoyment in surprising me combined with the good food and bracing coffee had a good effect on me.

"I had a couple of these sandwiches earlier today and they weren't nearly this good---must be you company!"

"That's nice to hear, John, but it's enough that you supplied the meal, you don't have to pay me compliments as well! Here I didn't even tell you how handsome you looked last night, all dressed up for the party! I'm glad you at least took time to change after church tonight, instead of rushing into town on my behalf still wearing your suit."

"I didn't change. We're very casual on Sunday nights."

"I certainly approve---but I'd bet your father wouldn't!"

John grinned. "We do a lot of things he doesn't know about. But I wouldn't change, people like the way we do things now."

"Good!"

"Feeling better?"

"Yes---thank you so much for coming, John, it's been a pretty bad day. This has been by far the best part of it!"

"Whenever you want to tell me about it---go ahead."

I took a deep breath, suddenly nervous again. "It's almost too much to unload onto anyone---I feel guilty asking you to listen."

John stretched his long legs and settled back in his chair. I walked about the room. "John, around noon, Rex came to the shop to talk to me and I found out just what father has told him about me and Fox Hollow---" as I went on John's face turned dark with a fine line of white around his mouth. I stopped, shocked at the anger he could show without uttering even one word.

"Has your father made this---offer---to anyone besides Rex and Mitch?" John's words were hard and clipped.

"No---I'm sure not, but I suspect you are the one he'll approach next." I sat down and made an effort to speak normally. "There's more, John. Father told me this afternoon that Claudette was not my mother---Megan is---he let it slip---"

"Wait! What? Your mother, Claudette --- your mother, Claudette is not your---mother?" John asked in shock.

"Father assumed Megan had told me long ago! I can get used to that, in time---but what hurt the most was when he said I killed little Nolan by not staying with him when I was told to watch him---that I let him fall down the stairs!"

John knelt by my chair and held my hands tightly.

"To learn that for all these years everyone at Fox Hollow has thought I let him fall! But I didn't---I was not told to take care of him or I would have done it! I loved Nolan! But what can I do now to change anyone's mind?"

"Someone neglected to watch Nolan---either Bertha or Claudette, and you were the only one they could blame for their carelessness."

"Do you really believe it wasn't my fault?"

"You are too honest to tell me about it if it had in any way been your fault!"

"I don't know if I am or not, John!"

"Admitting that only proves it---how much more honest can one be?" He grinned as he spoke, then stood up, pulling me up beside him. "I'm sorry your homecoming had to be such an unhappy one"

"Oh, I'll manage, having you to talk to helps. Thanks again for coming---and for supper!"

"There isn't much we can do about Thomas blaming you for Nolan's death---"

"I know, I guess only time can take care of that. Time will also settle how Megan and I react to each other now that I know the truth. It's Rex that scares me the most---Mitch is no problem. It's plain he's not interested in me or any part of father's offer, but Rex---"

"Rex is the only thing I can really do something about, Ellen, and I already have a possible solution. Talk to your father again, you both were under a lot of strain today. Make sure you want to stay here, and if you do, then we'll talk about my idea. If you'll be all right, I'll go now and check on dad."

"I'm fine. And if Rex is as persistent the next time I see him, I'll want to hear your idea. Thanks again for coming."

Later, as I prepared for bed, I was relieved to find I was feeling better. John had reacted so matter-of-factly that I could almost believe it would all work out. He'd certainly changed from the awkward boy of so long ago!

I turned on the television. A distraction would help until I felt sleepy. But I saw Rex's face again---he frighten me, yet what could he really do---his words ran through my mind---*this is how it's going to be Ellen, one way or another, we're going to be married*! How did he think he could force me to marry him---was there some plan he and father had that I knew nothing about---but my own father--- surely he couldn't be a party to something so unfeeling! But my own father is convinced I killed his son!

I'd try talking to father again, and if nothing changed, then I'd consider John's plan---whatever it might be!

And Megan---*Megan is my mother*---I shut out all other thoughts and repeated those words. In spite of the bitterness I felt at having been deceived, a little shiver of gladness ran through me. The woman I'd always admired above everyone I ever knew was my mother! For just this one moment, knowing that was enough.

But when morning came, I no longer felt so patient. I left the motel early enough to be certain of seeing father in case he would be leaving Fox Hollow on any business errands.

As I pulled up in front of the house, I saw him heading toward the stables. Reminding myself not to lose my temper I hurried to catch up.

He looked none too pleased as I came up beside him. "Figured I'd be seeing you sometime today. Out a bit early, aren't you?"

"I have things to do, so early seemed best. Let's go where we can talk. There are things we must settle."

"All right. But I'm selling a couple of horse this morning, so I haven't much time."

The sun was already warm on our backs as I followed him to a nearby pasture. The dew was still heavy on the shaded grass and my shoes were wet before we reached the wooden fence.

"This was old Bugle's pasture---do you remember him?"

I nodded.

"I loved that horse; he was a great hunter---these horses are of his linage---the only ones I put in here."

He seemed in an oddly reminiscent mood and it took me by surprise. I could deal with his indifference, even his anger, but we were strangers to one another in sharing anything more---I wanted to keep to familiar ground, I could not afford to weaken now.

"I'll get right to the point---I want you to stop completely this nonsense of encouraging Rex where I'm concerned! I want your word that you'll stop meddling!"

"Why, Ellen, I'm afraid it'd do no good for me to give my word as to what Rex will or won't do! Not that I wouldn't like to, but the idea is already in Rex's mind and he seems to like it! It's simply too late for me to step in!" He shrugged and smiled with maddening innocence.

"All right if you want to play it that way." I plunged on, still trying to keep my temper. "I want to know about you Megan---why didn't you marry her---did you even offer to, or was she just another roll in the hay?"

His face set suddenly, as if a mask had covered it. I wondered if he was trying to hold his own temper for a change!

"Ellen, we never intended for anything to happen between us! I knew Charles loved her, but Megan and I---it was something I can't explain---I loved her from the first time I saw her, even though I knew it was impossible. I was engaged to Claudette and Charles was my brother---"

"And let's not forget Claudette's money---that was the real reason you wouldn't marry Megan---even though she was pregnant!"

"I didn't know---" He practically groaned the words. "I didn't know until it was too late, I'd married Claudette!"

"For her money!"

"Yes. I paid for that; I'm still paying."

"How sad for you! You had Claudette and her money, you had Fox Hollow, you even had me! How you suffered! You had it all and Megan had nothing---how did you manage that?" It felt good, letting my bitterness pour into words.

"Claudette was---we were expecting a baby---"

"Quite the stud, weren't you?"

He went on, ignoring my interruption. "Claudette didn't know about Megan and me. Charles loved Megan enough to marry her even after she told him the truth. He had a construction job in the summers that had paid for his schooling, he was finishing it up when an accident at the site killed him and one other worker. After that, Megan went back to North Carolina.

"She had a good excuse to leave, her father was ill and needed her. Claudette considered Megan her friend, and when it was close to Megan's time, Claudette wanted to be with her. But Claudette had a miscarriage while in Wilmington, she wasn't strong that way, as we were to learn. I flew down to be with her and in the meantime, you were born.

"Claudette and I brought you back to Fox Hollow with us, as Megan was fighting to save her father's business---she couldn't do that and take care of you too. It was our agreement that you would stay here until she was on her feet financially. She felt it was best for you to be cared for by us rather than hire a stranger, which she could not really afford to do. She was too proud to take a dime from me, and I offered---more than once! Megan wanted you to have a normal life until she could take you herself. It was only to be for a short time."

"Then what happened---how did it turn into years?"

He turned away from me and looked toward the creek. "People naturally assumed you were Claudette's baby---she was expecting a child when she left and she returned with a newborn daughter. We'd been told Claudette should not attempt to have another child and it was in my mind then to keep you. I thought Megan might see you were better off here and agree. But Claudette found out you were my child and not Charles'."

"How did she learn the truth?" I was hardly breathing, amazed to hear I had been the center of such a drama.

"She overheard me tell Megan that as long as you were living in my house, since I was your father and legally named as such, it would be kidnapping if Megan should try to take you with her. I told her I'd take her to court and she'd lose---she had no home to offer you, not with a father and mother like you had here."

"And Megan believed you?"

"I said I'd checked the law thoroughly---I hadn't I was bluffing---I always expected her to take you. For some reason I've never figured out, she didn't."

"You'd gladly given me up if you'd had sons---then you wouldn't nave needed me for anything!"

"No. Even after Nolan was born, I intended to keep you. I wouldn't have let you go if I'd had ten sons! You were my only hold on Megan---if she took you, I was afraid I'd never see her again and I lived for that!"

"If Megan wanted you to know the truth, don't you think she'd have told you herself? Maybe she's tired of worrying about you, maybe she'd like to get on with her own life without feeling anymore obligation to you!"

His words cut through me and I felt the sting of tears.

"Rex is here, I see. I think we've said enough, and I've got horse to sell."

"You're selling to Rex---what does he want with horse?"

"What do I care---he's paying a good price and I want rid of a couple! Come ask him if you're interested."

"I've no wish to see Rex---I'm going to a walk!"

"I think that's wise. You're too upset to be civil to anyone. Go cool off."

He walked briskly away and I plunged off toward the creek. Our conversation had changed nothing as far as my father was concerned, but it had settled something for me. I crossed the footbridge and was up the hill before I stopped.

I turned to my left going along the road to Fox Hollow, walking slowly now, absently plucking burrs from my jeans. This would bring me back around to my car without having to pass the stables. It was farther, but it was just as well, I wanted to think about Megan and all the things father had told me---I thought he was right---there had to be some reason besides his threats that made Megan leave me at Fox Hollow. The obvious answer being that she had not wanted the responsibility of a small child. Would I ever know the entire truth?

I caught the sound of a motor and hurriedly crossed the road where a thicket offered protection---if it was Rex, I didn't want to be seen. I was on his property now, I realized, on this side of the road where Flagg property stopped, Rex's began.

I waited. Hearing nothing more, I started cautiously on, feeling a need to stay near cover. Just as I was about to round a curve, I heard the slamming of car doors and voices. I moved into the brush and went carefully on. There was a lane ahead, the sounds had come from there.

I was as close now as I dared to go, but it was close enough to see Rex and two other men and hear most of what they said. I knew what was going on as soon as I saw the large horse van. Rex's pickup truck pulling a double horse trailer was parked beside it. The men were unloading the two horses Rex had just bought from my father.

Feeling ill, I sat down on an old log---Fox Hollow horses were being sold as food for the European market---it was a practice despised by horse owners. Anyone dealing with these men, butchers was one of the more polite terms for them, would find themselves outcasts if it became known. The butchers themselves would soon be forced to leave the county, as in their own ways the local horse owners made certain it was too uncomfortable for them to remain.

But Rex would not be able to resist the quick profit---a horse brought two to three times the price from these men, and no questions asked as to its age or health!

Horse-butchers like these always turned up at horse shows and sale barns, but they were watched for and the local people took delight in sending them all over the surrounding counties in search of non-existent horses supposedly for sale at bargain prices. The experienced butcher found a go-between, like Rex, and made his deals hidden from view.

Did father know why Rex bought his horses? I couldn't believe he did---the log I was sitting upon was more rotted than I'd thought, and it gave way, sending me sideways into a tangle of brush and briars. I stayed still waiting to see if the men had heard the slight commotion.

Only Rex seemed to have heard anything, and he merely glanced around a moment before taking his wallet out and stuffing into it the money offered by the men. Then he started his truck and turned out onto the road. I waited until the others left, then hurried across the road back onto Jordane land.

When at last I reached the stables, father as not to be found. I'd tell Ersey, that would be best anyway! I found him currying a young mare, talking gently as he worked.

"Ersey---" I was so out of breath I sank down onto a bench beside the stall.

"What's the matter---if you're lookin' for your father, he's gone, I 'spect for the rest of the day."

"No, that's good---I want to tell you---Ersey, those horses Rex bought this morning---he's sold them to a couple of horse-butchers, I saw him! They met in the lane that goes back to the barn on the Post place!"

Ersey straightened slowly and came out of the stall. "Those horses was born and raised right here at Fox Hollow---they're gonna wind up on some supper table in France? You real sure who he was sellin' to?"

"I'm sure---no one else hides to do business---Rex hardly bothered to get out of sight of Fox Hollow!"

"I always knowed Rex Post was no good---always knowed it! Told Bertha so more than once---you reckon your---reckon anyone else know he's doin' this?"

"I can't honestly say, Ersey, when it comes to making money, I don't think father has many scruples---but I don't think he knows why Rex bought his horses."

"Well, Rex won't buy no more---not in this county or any close to it---been more than one fella put out of that business!"

"I'm glad to hear that, I can't bear to think of Rex getting any more of our horses!"

"I owe you a favor, Ellen, I won't forget it, neither!"

I left; glad I could leave the situation to Ersey. I knew

he loved caring for father's horses; he considered each one of them his own. He would stop Rex's little sideline. Maybe Rex would even leave---I tried not to count on that, but just the thought cheered me as I drove into town.

Back in my room, I showered and changed, anxious to get to the shop.

In the small room off the office, I found Rachel, sorting through a box of hangers.

"Well! Hi, Ellen, I wondered where you were! The painters were here when I arrived, it's going to look great! These hangers are all mixed up---pants hangers and blouse hangers and broken hangers---"

I was glad she wasn't paying any attention to me; I hadn't expected her to be in yet and I didn't want her to start talking about Rex, her usual subject.

"Oh, and Ellen, there's some good news for you, I think. Mrs. Birkdale called. She's wondering if you still need a place to live, seems the couple that she thought was going to rent her house has backed out. She's all upset, afraid this will delay their trip. She wants you to call right away if you're interested."

"I sure am! I'm sick of that motel room!"

After returning the call, I drove out to the Birkdale home at once. It was a brick bungalow on the North edge of town.

"Miss Jordane, this is wonderful! We won't rent to just anyone---we're leaving our furniture and you have to be so careful about people! But we won't have a worry with you here!"

I escaped to my car, leaving her smiling and waving. I'd move in in two days---finding an apartment was one problem off my list.

Late Wednesday afternoon, I gladly put the shop records away. It had been a tiring day. Megan had called that morning for a progress report. She had sounded distant, and I'd felt so strange I was sure I hadn't been myself, either. Megan had not seemed to notice, however, and kept the conversation short.

I turned to Rachel. "Let's call it a day, we've done a

lot. Want a ride home?"

"Thanks, but Rex is coming by---I haven't had a chance to tell you---we're going out on the town, first time in a while---dinner and dancing!"

I looked away, pretending to sort papers. "Somewhere here in town?"

"Oh, no---we're going to Indianapolis, the Indiana Roof, no less! Say, had you heard they're going to tear that place down before much longer---some new office building going up."

"That's sad. It's been a famous landmark for a long time. Megan and Charles used to go there when they were dating---she said they had to save up for it, but it was the place to go! Hope it doesn't rain since you have such a nice evening ahead, it's looking as if it might."

"It won't dampen our good time if it does! Rex says we're celebrating---seems he came into a nice bit of money from one of his deals."

I thought of the horses. *I hope he chokes on his steak!* I decided I'd leave at once; I had no desire to see Rex!

"You can lock up, Rachel, have fun tonight---I'll see you tomorrow!"

I hurried around the corner to my car. "Why little Foxey-Locksey---what's your rush---you're always in such a hurry!" Rex was suddenly beside me, grinning in a way I found insulting.

"Rachel is inside, waiting for you---and I am in a hurry!" I reached for the car door. He put his hand over mine.

"Then I'll open the door for you! Why, Ellen, what a nasty scratch! That's going to take some time to heal---how did that happen? A broken hanger, or a briar, maybe? Been in the woods lately?" He raised an eyebrow mockingly.

I got in the car and slammed the door. Without looking back, I knew he still stood there, watching---I could feel it. I also knew he had heard me in the woods, but he hadn't seen me---he'd seen my car at Fox Hollow that day, but he was only guessing that I'd seen him.

Going home to a house again was a pleasant change. I

chose the bedroom Mrs. Birkdale had used as a guest room and hung my clothes in the large closet.

I walked down the hall to the living room. Three walls were paneled, the other was entirely brick with a large fireplace. The floor was a glossy hardwood with a braided rug. The kitchen was small, with a breakfast nook. There was a dining room with a glass-front china cabinet showing off Mrs. Birkdale's candlestick collection. One small room off the living room held a beautiful piano, a desk, a small sofa and two occasional chairs. The bay window looked out on the patio and yard---it was a charming room and I wondered who had played the piano, I'd have bet it wasn't Mrs. Birkdale---her hands were too flighty!

The house was decorated and furnished in a rather outdated style that was to me, part of its charm. It was very comfortable and had a settled feeling that I liked.

I was expecting John later, so I checked the kitchen for supplies and left for the grocery with a long list.

I nearly had things put away when I heard his car. "Come on in John, how about this place? Sure beats the motel!"

"You were lucky to get it---do you know how hard it is to find something for rent in a college town?"

"I know but this is an unusual situation. The Birkdale's would only rent to someone they knew, and they don't really know how long they'll be away---not many people are interested in such uncertain terms."

"It's certainly nice---you know where the fuse box is and all that?"

"Yes, Mr. Birkdale was quite thorough."

"How are things going with you otherwise---did you get things straightened out with your father?"

I shook my head. "Things are worse if anything. And I've found out Rex is buying horses and selling to butchers! I saw him sell two of father's horses Monday. He and Rachel are out tonight, celebrating his little windfall."

"Does Rex know you saw him?"

"He let me know this afternoon that he suspects, but that's all. I'm sure Rachel doesn't know what he's doing."

"In a way, I wish she did. Maybe then she'd stay away from him." John looked so unhappy as he spoke, I couldn't help feeling sorry for him.

"John, you have enough worries of your own without listening to mine! Come on, let me show you the house, then we'll have a quick bite. I'll open a can of something---I'm not much of a cook, so don't over expect!"

"This is the room I like." John opened the piano, sat down and ran his fingers over the keys.

"I didn't know you could play---don't stop!"

"Maybe later." He closed it and went to the window. "Ellen, I think it's about time we talked about what you're going to do---obviously you plan to stay here, so you have to face this problem with Rex."

"I know, it's not as if I could go to the police for help---what could I say---Rex kissed me, and my father wants him to marry me? Even if I told them about the telephone call and the note, they'd not take any of it seriously, not until something drastic happened---and that could be too late to be of help to me!" I had never put that thought into words before---saying it aloud gave me a chill.

"There's been a note? You didn't tell me!"

"I found it at the shop, Sunday morning, and then there was that incident with Rex and all the things father told me---it just didn't seem important after all that."

"Ellen, of course it's important!" He sounded angry. "Now come sit down and listen to what I'm going to say---hear it all before you answer." We sat down and John moved his chair to face me. "This is so simple and clear in my mind, but I know it's going to be hard for you to even consider it, at first, so take time to think it over before you say anything."

I nodded, trying to imagine what he was going to say.

"You need protection, at least for a time, from Rex and your father's interference and from whoever is behind these threats. You have to convince Rex you're out of his reach and show everyone you have no intention of moving into Fox Hollow. You need a husband and I need a wife, temporarily, to satisfy my father for however long he has left---I've been told perhaps a year under good conditions. I want to do anything I can to help give him that year!

"Ellen, if we were to marry, and I mean under strictly plutonic conditions---your problems and mine would be solved! I can assure you I'd keep my word, under those circumstances an annulment would be granted and you could take your maiden name again."

I swallowed, trying to think what to say---but I could only think of Mitch---how could I even consider marriage with John, even in the way he was suggesting---but Mitch loves Denise, not me, I'll never have Mitch---

"If you should agree, I'll talk to the deacons and elders of the church first, then father---no one would be too surprised. We've known each other since childhood. We could be married soon, a simple ceremony---with father ill, no one would expect a long engagement or a big wedding, or even a honeymoon trip afterward, naturally I wouldn't want to be away."

"John, I---I don't know what to say!"

"You do believe me when I say we'd be married in name only?"

I nodded. "But a minister's wife---there are so many duties, so much is expected ---I couldn't do those things, attend all those ladies' meetings, be on committees---"

"No problem, our congregation is on the small side, there is little of that and you'll be busy with your shop, people would understand."

"But I can't play the piano, and I sound like a rusty gate when I sing---I've never known a minister's wife who couldn't play and sing well!"

John put his head back and laughed. "One pianist in the house is sufficient, and I can sing loudly enough for both of us!" He went to the piano and began playing Rhapsody In Blue, his touch was light and sure, but I sensed a restraint about him, in the way he held his body and the way he played as well.

I was glad of the chance to study him. This man---this boy I used to know---has asked me to marry him! What can I say to him? Now I longed to talk to Megan!

Megan---who was my mother but had not wanted me

to know---for the first time I felt a sadness in thinking about her. It must have shown on my face, for after a quick glance at me John broke into Roll Out the Barrel, singing with exuberance!

I couldn't help laughing. He stopped and turned to face me.

"Ellen, I can't love you, not as a man ordinarily loves the girl he marries, but I can be here when you need someone to talk with, I want to help with your problems and be sure you're never lonely---it wouldn't be for too long a time. Some people are married for years and have none of these things between them!"

Even from across the room I saw the sincerity in his eyes, now midnight blue as they held my gaze. His voice was rich and low, pleading with me to understand. "You are dear to me, Ellen."

Only Megan had ever spoken so to me and I was deeply touched. I knew that if I agreed it would be just as John said. I didn't doubt that he was being totally honest with me---even more so than Megan had been---a painful truth for me to admit!

"Thank you, John. I appreciate what you are offering, and your caring---you are a good friend---a good person." I got up and walked to the piano bench. "I will think about this and we'll talk about it again, soon. Now, let's go to the kitchen---you've sung for your supper---and very well , too!"

Seven

It had rained during the night, a hard, steady rain that kept time with the incessant pounding in my temples. Hours of weighing what John had proposed had produced a headache that was only now beginning to ease.

I poured a last cup of coffee, perked strong and rich---it was the only culinary ability I could claim, but it was, I consoled myself, a very important one!

Minutes later I was backing out the drive, already thinking how nice it would be to come home to this house. For the moment, that pleasant prospect made me forget that I looked just the way I felt---tired and a bit too pale in spite of my carefully applied make-up.

I reached the shop just as the painters arrived. Their progress had been rapid and if things continued to do well the shop would be ready to re-open even sooner than I'd hoped. *Just that much sooner I can show father I can do something right*---now it was all the more important that I not fail, I wanted Megan to finally feel proud of me. Perhaps then she would want to tell me herself that I was her daughter.

"Well, Miss Jordane, we'll be out of your way by noon---just got to hang this one wall of paper. Then they can get your carpet down---people won't know this place!"

"Good! I'm delighted with it." It was true, people wouldn't recognize it---a little shiver of pride ran through me, followed immediately by the question, would Megan like it?

It was too late now to change my mind---the roll of paper was on a long table being measured and cut. Yesterday I had been sure of the decorator's choice---but today---

On impulse, I stepped out the front door. The newly done store front propped up my sagging confidence. The old awning was gone and the old name removed, the once dark grey bricks now wore a much lighter, softer grey. The window was set off by cream shutters and long shutters of the same color outlined a new door painted wedgewood blue. And there was the new name---Paige Two---

"Hello Ellen."

Totally engrossed, I had paid no attention to the few people passing by.

"Mitch! I didn't see you---" I knew my smile was becoming a rather foolish grin anyone could read, but I couldn't seem to stop it. The soaring feeling he always caused spilled through me. I felt a slight easing of the tightness that had been clamped inside me the past several days.

The warming in his eyes touched me even more than his answering smile. But I knew I had to stop the things I was suddenly feeling---hadn't I made this mistake just a few days ago?

"Mitch, would you like to come in? It isn't finished, of course, but you can have a preview."

"May I be included?"

The voice played like windchimes touched by a mischievous breeze. I knew without turning it was Denise. I watched Mitch's eyes as they left my face to look at her, was I wrong, or did a little of the warmth I'd enjoyed die away.

Slowly, I turned to face her. I was wrong. No man could look at Denise without his interest quickening! She was smiling politely, looking serene and lovely in expensively tailored butter-cream yellow slacks and blazer with a navy shirt. Her blond hair was tied back with a navy and yellow striped scarf.

She removed her sunglasses. Rachel had been right about those eyes, I thought, they were an unusual shade, very violet. They regarded me with a hint of amusement.

"Ellen, this is Denise Graham---Ellen Jordane."

"Hello, Ellen, Mitch has spoken of you."

Was there triumph in her smile? "I'm glad to meet you, Denise, and, of course, I'd like to show you both the shop, if you've time."

"Well, we'd love to see it, Ellen, but we're taking my car to the garage." She waved in the general direction of the cars parked along the street. "Silly thing has needed first one thing then another fixed since I bought it last month---I don't think I'll keep it if one more thing goes wrong!" She spoke with the detached amusement of one unused to owning anything with a flaw. It stirred an unreasonable amount of dislike in me for such a trivial thing.

"We've plenty of time, Denise, and Ellen did invite me to stop by. When I saw her standing out here, I decided if she had time for loitering, she wasn't too busy for company!"

Denise shrugged in a gesture that plainly said, if we must, we must! As Mitch opened the door, she moved through ahead of me and stood to one side, making it plain she expected the tour to be short.

"Mitch, have you seen Megan's shop before?"

"I must admit, this is the first time, but there's enough of the old left to see how much you're improving it."

I looked at the dull green, tiled floor. "The brown carpet will do wonders."

"Brown? I should think beige would tie in better with the wall covering, certainly it would lend a more elegant effect!" Denise had not moved from her place just inside the door.

The flicker of annoyance I saw cross Mitch's face gave me the courage to defend my choice.

"I agree beige would be lovely, Denise, but I have to be practical. Brown will stand the traffic better." I faced the cool violet gaze as it raked over me, reminding me I came in a poor second best to its owner.

"Of course. I can see you are one of those people who value practicality above all else!" Her gaze roved about the shop. "I doubt if I'll see it when it's completed, but I'm sure it will be quite nice." Her too bright voice managed to convey her doubts in the matter even as she spoke and I felt a hot flood of resentment. So, this was the charming Denise---well, I was definitely not charmed!

"Tell you what---" she continued in the same bright, bell-like voice that was beginning to set my teeth on edge, "---I'll run on and leave my car at the garage, they promised me the loan of that little sports job I admired, so I'll be back in a flash!"

I saw fond tolerance in the smile she threw at Mitch. The careless little wave in my direction told me she was sure there was no risk in leaving us along. I remembered my vow to make Mitch forget Denise the next time we were alone---how foolish to have ever thought that might be possible!

Her nearly perfect presence lingered, seeming to have as strong an effect on me as had Denise herself---I'd felt completely un-equal to the occasion. I was sure Mitch had found me as lacking as I found myself.

"Ellen, can we sit down somewhere and talk?"

"The office is a bit of a mess, but there are chairs." I turned and bumped into the corner of the table holding the wallpaper. Mitch reached out to steady me. The mere touch of his hand on my arm was enough to make me wish we were alone again in the cedar grove, before I knew about Denise---when I thought Mitch was still here for me!

I closed the office door and forced myself to look at something, anything, other than Mitch.

"Congratulations Mitch, Denise is lovely. You're very fortunate."

"Your congratulations are premature, Ellen." His reply was in an even, almost disinterested tone. I could feel him waiting for me to look at him.

"Denise said she wouldn't be here when the shop is finished---is she going away?"

"She's going home this week. It happens I have a seminar to attend in Philadelphia so I'm leaving tomorrow. While I'm there she and I will get things cleared up, I feel I should talk to her parents myself."

"Of course! She'll want you to meet her family and friends!" The words flew out sounding small and mean. "I'm sorry, Mitch, I didn't mean to sound like that." Now I met his gaze and saw again that flicker of some banked emotion that now and then glowed there.

"Ellen, I want to tell you what I started to explain the night I took you home from the party. There are a lot of things I want to tell you---"

"If it's about you and Denise you needn't. I really think I've finally grasped the situation!" I had given up trying to remain aloof.

He shook his head. "That isn't what I mean, although it's part of it---this isn't a good place to talk , but it seems this will be our only chance for a while. Ellen, over the years I've heard all about the day your father sent you away---about the attempt to sabotage that fox hunt---I couldn't believe you and Rex and John cooking up something like that!"

"It was stupid---but I wanted to get even with father for shooting my dog and John and Rex thought it would be an adventure, then there was the accident---"

"But Ellen, Claudette had been drinking, everyone knew it---it was obvious that caused her fall! It wasn't due to any of the things Rex and John had set up, so why was your father so hard on you?"

"Something else he thought I had done was the real cause of his anger toward me, but that's another story and it's too late for me to expect father to change his ideas about me."

"Ellen," his voice was low and I more felt than heard the anger in it. "I know you've had a lot of pressures put on you since you came back and the last thing I want to do is to add to them---but there are things I must talk to you about, things you have to know!"

I looked at the fine lines his face already held from hours spent in the sun and wind. I could barely keep from reaching out and tracing them---perhaps I even moved to touch them, for his strong, browned hands suddenly held my own firmly.

"Ellen, I didn't know you were coming back---I thought you'd forgotten about Fox Hollow---and me---"

"Ellen, are you back here?"

It was Rachel's voice. I pulled my hands from Mitch as she came through the door.

"Well, hello, Mitch! Hi Ellen! Giving tours already?"

"Hello, Rachel." Mitch answered. "Ellen, I've taken enough of your time, we'll talk again."

The door barely closed behind him before Rachel rushed to speak. "Something awful happened last night, Ellen---that big barn on Rex's property has burned! Rex says there's hardly any of it still standing!"

There was no need to wonder if Rachel had sensed the tension between Mitch and myself, she was too caught up in her news.

"Did lightning strike it?"

"No." Rachel shook her head emphatically. "Rex is certain the fire was set by someone."

"Why---how could he know that?"

"Because he was renting stall space and the horses were let out---he's sure if lightning had caused the fire the horses would have died from the smoke, if not the flames. Someone let them out, then started the fire, there's just no doubt in his mind!"

"I just don't see how he can be so certain." But to myself I thought that Ersey had not let any grass grow under his feet, he was serious about stopping Rex.

"Ellen, Rex says someone has it in for him---he says whoever did it has a grudge against him. I think he knows who it was and he'll try to get even---it scares me, you never know what Rex will do!"

I sank into the same chair I'd left only moments ago, my head was starting to ache again, I had to stop Rachel from talking about Rex! "There's nothing to gain by your worrying, Rachel, I'm sure Rex was insured---by the way, I finally met Denise Graham."

"Oh? And what did you think of her?" Rachel quickly sat down across from me, looking eager for my reply.

"She is all you said, and more! I've never felt more of a klutz in my life! My feet were suddenly twice their size, I bumped something every time I moved---it was a depressing experience!"

Rachel laughed, "Ellen, you always cheer me up! So I'm going to do something for you in return. I'm going to clean this office and put it in perfect order, so take your bookwork home and give me room!"

I shrugged, puzzled by her change of mood. "If you really want to, that would be great. Just call me if the carpet people come."

Grateful for the chance to be alone, I headed for the sanctuary of the Birkdale's house. Sunshine was smoothing away all trace of last night's storm, but for all its warmth it could not touch the cold core of fear Rachel's words formed in me! *Rex will get even; you never know what Rex will do!*

But he couldn't think I was responsible, at least this would give him something to think about besides me! That thought made me relax somewhat, and my mind turned to Mitch.

What had he wanted to tell me---now I would probably never know, he was leaving tomorrow for Philadelphia. I felt sure if Denise had her way they would both remain there.

My spirits were low as I turned into the drive. I longed for the comfort of a long talk with Megan---but now she was just as far out of my reach as Mitch. In telling me the truth, father had placed a barrier between me and Megan I was afraid to cross. I was afraid to risk finding I was not as welcome as her daughter as I'd been as her niece.

Unlocking the kitchen door, I stepped inside and stood a moment, listening. There was only silence and I shrugged off my sudden case of jitters. I'd change into comfortable clothes and get at my work.

As I undressed, I thought how considerate Rachel was to volunteer tackling the office---she was interested in everything about the shop. I stood in my slip, wondering if I'd unpacked the shirt I wanted.

"Maybe I'd better let you know you're not alone!" The voice came from the doorway behind me.

I spun around to see Rex grinning at me. "How dare you break into my house!" I snatched my robe from a chair and scrambled into it. "If you don't stop hounding me---"

"Now, calm yourself! I didn't break in---you didn't lock the kitchen door just now, so I simply walked in! Now you can also save me the trouble of searching the place. Just hand over that film."

"What?" Rex was watching me with none of the amusement of a moment earlier. For the first time I noticed the dirt on his face and hands. He moved closer and I caught the acrid tang of smoke and damp ashes clinging to his clothes.

"Ellen, I'm tired, I want a bath and clean clothes and I want that film! I know you saw me sell your old man's horses to those butchers. You always took your camera to the woods when you were a kid, and just in case you had it that day, I want the film---I don't need that kind of proof shown to the local gentry! Rumors are bad enough; they were enough to get my barn burned and to force me to leave town until a few irate horse lovers cool off!"

"There's only my little camera, it's all I brought back with me and it isn't loaded. I wasn't at Fox Hollow for pleasure. I had an argument with father and I took a walk to cool off, that's how I happened to see you." I thought it best to admit the truth. I met his eyes steadily. "When are you leaving town?"

He grinned and put his hand under my chin, tipping my head back to look in my eyes. "I won't be away long, two, maybe three weeks, I have some business matters here and there I need to attend to, anyway. But I do believe you about the camera."

I stepped backward to escape is touch. "Does Rachel know you're leaving?"

"She's no problem. Rachel's used to me coming and going. And when I get back, she's going to have something else to get used to."

"What do you mean?"

"You and me, of course! Going to be a wedding---as big or as small as you want, won't matter to me, but there's going to be one, no way around it!"

I was at a loss for words strong enough to voice my disgust, I stood still, fighting the impulse to fly at him and scratch the smug leer off his face.

"Accept it, Ellen, you're like a fox in a trap!"

I sat down on the edge of the bed. The kitchen door slammed. He was gone. *You're like a fox in a trap*---the words in the note had said the same thing---and I was feeling very much like a hunted animal! But the trap had not closed yet---there was still time to escape! Or would I just be exchanging one kind of trap for another?

No! The answer was quick. I believed John, and I would be glad to be helping him in return. Mitch was lost to me; I was sure he would never back out of his "understanding" with Denise. Nor had he shown any sign that he wanted to ---not really---he had been kind and concerned, that was all.

And Megan, what would she say about all this---I knew she would have only to say, "Ellen, come home to me!" and I would want to go---but I couldn't leave the shop. Megan was depending on me now, and my father would never respect me if I were to give up and run.

My fear of Rex was growing, but there was still an out----if I could summon the nerve to take it!

Eight

"Ellen, dear, you're so nervous---but of course brides always are!" Mrs. Flagg's smile trembled as she patted my hand. I hoped fervently she wouldn't cry.

"I want to say again how happy we all are about this wedding." She went on, sounding as if she could barely believe what was about to happen. I was having trouble believing it myself. "This is the first time in weeks Isaac has had the will to get out of the house, and now here he is---waiting to see his son married! Well, I'll go now, I'm sure you'd like a minute to be alone."

"Thank you, Mrs. Flagg." Were those strained, awkward sounding words mine? My nerves crackled under my skin. She was right, I did want some time alone---*to do what---change your mind? Because of Mitch? He's happy with Denise!*

It was too late now to wonder if this was a mistake---no one else thought it was. The Flagg's had been elated at the news; Rachel had been right about their reaction. No obstacles had been put in our way. John had extended a verbal invitation to the congregation and in only two weeks everything was arranged.

My father had been jubilant, taking it for granted that John and I would soon move to Fox Hollow. He was constantly pointing out the advantages.

Bertha had just grinned and said nothing. She seemed so unconcerned that I wondered if she somehow knew there would be no grandchildren for father.

And Megan---I had puzzled over her reaction all through the busy days of re-opening the shop. When I'd called her to tell her how well the first week of business had gone, I could tell she was pleased, yet at the same time she'd seemed oddly preoccupied. When I'd gone on to tell her John and I were being married, she had sounded openly relieved not even questioning the suddenness of it.

But Megan was not here for my wedding, she'd given some excuse I'd hardly heard in my hurt at her seeming disinterest. Perhaps father had guessed the truth the day he'd so coldly said Megan had no wish to feel responsible for me any longer!

Nor would she have to---today would change everything! And just in time---Rex was due back. When Rachel had shared that news with me, she'd been so happy and exited she hadn't noticed my reaction was one of pure alarm. But our conversation that day had lent strength and desperation to my resolve. I remembered her exact words---

"Rex will be back just any day now---he even told me to ask you if any of our dresses would do for a bride to wear---he's finally ready to get married! Can you believe it? He's going to have to ask me in a more romantic way than this, but I'm sure he will!"

"Did you tell him about John and me?"

"No, I'm not sure just what day he'll be back, so if he's back intime he can attend, if not---" she shrugged.

I'd known then Rex was deadly serious---if he could be so cruel to Rachel, letting her think he intended to marry her while he planned to---to---I had never been able to finish that thought, but I'd known I could not back out, I had to marry John!

Rachel opened the door. "It's time---everyone's here, and I do mean everyone! The church is packed!" She came in and picked up my bouquet. "Ellen, I'm grateful to you, you're going to change John's life." Her eyes were moist as she handed me the flowers.

I forced a smile, "I'm ready."

At the very moment Rachel and I were in place, the wedding march began and everyone stood, turning toward us I clutched a ragged breath and started down the aisle, now a long plank running through a sea of curious faces.

I saw John, standing with his best man whom I'd met only last night at our brief rehearsal. The minister performing our ceremony was a stranger to me also, but Reverend Stewart was a good friend of John's and I'd like him immediately.

Just a few more steps---I dared a quick glance at John and felt a zig-zag of shock run through me. As if unaware of all who were watching, he was looking at me with such warmth and tender concern that I was totally unnerved!

This is wrong---John can't actually love me---does he?---oh dear heaven! A slight nudge from Rachel and I tightened my hold on my bouquet and took the final steps. Then John was at my side and a solemn voice began the ceremony.

Reverend Stewart knows---he knows we shouldn't be married---no---he couldn't---we have no choice---I have no choice!

From the corner of my eye, I could see Rachel, intent on each word---it was she wearing the look of a bride at my wedding.

I knew the ceremony itself would cause raised eyebrows. John and I had changed the wording considerably to avoid breaking promises we had no intention of keeping. I was sure we'd both be lectured by John's father as soon as he had the opportunity.

I had not asked my father to give me away, nor had he mentioned the break in tradition. I knew his only disappointment was in Megan's absence.

There was a pause---had I missed a cue---no---
Reverend Stewart had merely asked if anyone present
objected to this wedding taking place---the solemn voice
continued.

*So---did you think Mitch would suddenly appear and
whisk you away?* Woodenly I made my replies. John's
voice was strong and sure. Rachel took my bouquet as John
reached for my hand---the ring slid onto my finger and it was
over! John briefly touched his lips to mine; music filled the
space around us and we were moving up the aisle to the back
of the church.

"Are you alright, Ellen?" John whispered.

I searched his eyes as we stood in the receiving line.
"Yes, I'm sorry I was so nervous, I don't know what came
over me." It was only friendship and relief that I saw in his
face now.

John laughed and squeezed my arm. "This won't take
long. We'll be able to relax soon."

"Stop whispering you two, it isn't dignified!" Rachel
was all smiles. "Have you ever seen a more nervous bride? I
had to poke her with my elbow every time it as her turn to
speak!" She laughed at my dismay. "No, Ellen, I don't know
how, but you were just fine!"

There was no more time for conversation. The guests
were coming to greet us. I saw the fire in Reverend Flagg's
eyes when he looked at me and knew I'd been right about the
lecture we'd get.

Only when the line of well-wishers dwindled did I
notice John's parents were no longer beside us.

"Mom thought it best if they went back to the house."
Rachel lowered her voice so only John and I might hear.
"Dad did look a bit upset; I think it was all those changes in
your vows! Oh, and I'm to tell you both he wants to see you
as soon as you can get away from the reception. I think you
two are in trouble!" She grinned at the dark look John gave
her.

"I'll go look in on him for a second, this has been a
strain for him. I'll be right back, stay with Ellen, will you

Sis?"

"Of course, but hurry back. Ellen, did I see your father leave right after the ceremony?"

"Yes, the reception wouldn't interest him---only the wedding! Besides, he said he was expecting someone at Fox Hollow, probably about horses or hounds. I'm glad he went---he makes me nervous when he smiles so much---have you ever seen him act so nice to me?"

Rachel didn't answer. I glanced at her and saw her staring past me, her face a mixture of surprise and defiance.

I turned to look into the white-hot gaze of Rex Post. The anger that twisted his mouth and choked his voice made his words hiss like steam as he spoke. "If you think you've outsmarted me, you're a fool! I told you---one way or another---and I still mean it! This is only a delay, and you'll pay a high price for it, soon!" He looked at Rachel. "I'll talk to you later!" A few long strides and he was out the door.

"Well, well---don't guess I ever did see anyone so mad---was Rex teed off 'cause he wasn't invited?"

I turned back to find Bertha had been an interested observer. "Bertha, would you please go and tell them to start serving the refreshments, I know people are waiting." I wanted only to escape her probing eyes. "Sure, but ain't you gonna get pictures took and all that?"

"No. We're keeping it all very simple."

"Come along, Bertha, I'll go with you---John is coming, Ellen."

Rachel left the door where she'd been staring after Rex.

Hurriedly, I drew a few deep breaths and tried to get a grip on myself. And I did feel steadier when John came in.

"Mrs. Flagg, shall we attend our reception?"

I answered his smile and took his arm. "Was your father all right?"

"Yes. I spoke to mother, but she said he was better. She said she couldn't talk him out of seeing us."

"It won't take long, we'll let him get it off his mind. He'll rest better."

"Thank you, Ellen, for being so patent with him. I

have a surprise for you, a rather strange wedding gift---I'll show you when we leave the reception."

We cut the cake, drank punch and talked to everyone. Rachel was subdued and a little pale. She avoided meeting my eyes, but I felt her following my every move and I wondered if she had fully understood the motive behind Rex's violent words. If she didn't, she soon would---and what would she do then?

My unhappy thoughts were stilled by John's hand on my arm.

"We can leave now without being noticed, if you're ready."

I nodded and we slipped out of the door into the hallway. The ceremony had begun at two thirty, giving time after the morning church service for everyone to go home for their big Sunday dinners while the church was being decorated for the wedding. Now the late afternoon sun made darker green shadows cross the lawn and it was pleasant to be outside in the cooler air.

"May I see that surprise now?"

"Maybe you should wait until you've changed---it might ruin your dress."

I looked down at my ivory street-length dress. "It'll clean. I'm too curious to wait!"

"All right, just don't try to stick me with your cleaning bill!"

My spirits rose a bit as John pulled me toward the garage on the opposite side of his parent's house. He was in a lighthearted mood, more so than I'd seen him in all the time I'd been back. It was the first real pleasure I'd found in the entire day and I felt what we were doing could work after all!

"Wait right here!"

I stood until he reappeared, leading a black and tan Doberman pinscher.

"Oh! John---what a beautiful dog!" I held my hand out. The dog timidly sniffed it, wagging its stump of a tail.

"Ellen, I hope you don't think this is too strange, my giving you a dog---but I want you to have some protection around the house when I'm away!"

"I love it---I haven't had a dog since good old Braidy! Thank you, John. She needs a name---any idea?"

"She's only about eight months old, the breeder was happy to be rid of her. Seems she's too large for a female, too large to show or to breed---he didn't want that tendency passed on through her litters---he said he was tired of feeding her with nothing to gain so he was happy to sell her. She's sort of a female Samson, I guess!"

"Then let's call her Samantha---Sam for short, agreed?"

"That's fine! I'll put her back in the garage and we'll get that talk with father over."

Protection---well, it's not a bad idea, although I don't think Sam can handle Rex just yet---I'll have to tell John Rex is back, but not now, I'll wait and tell him later---

"Now, into the lion's den!"

While I knew John was teasing me, I felt he had given an accurate description of what we faced!

Mrs. Flagg seemed as nervous as I was. She spoke quick and low, not quite meeting our eyes. "Isaac is very upset, so it's best to just let him speak his mind without trying to---"

John patted her shoulder, "It'll be all right, don't worry I've been through this before and Ellen understands.

The three of us entered the bedroom. Heavy drapes were drawn across the window, making the room depressingly dim.

"Opal sit down. John and Ellen, come to me." The voice rumbled ominously from the bed. Mrs. Flagg obeyed, as did John and I, going to stand at the foot of the bed.

I looked at the man propped against a wall of pillows, a light blanket showing the outline of long, thin legs. *Who does he think he is---if my father was ever right about anything, it was in his opinion of this pompous old hypocrite!*

"I have never---never---been as disappointed as I am today!" The voice thundered out of the dry shell before us. "I must assume Ellen is responsible for that travesty, that mockery of the sacred vows a man and woman are commanded to exchange according to God's will! Ellen, you were poorly brought up, therefore ignorant of the folly this will bring upon the two of you---for you, John, there is no excuse! You let a woman's whims sway you, that will lead you down the path to damnation quicker than anything else! You must be strong, as I have been---it is your God given right to rule over your wife, that is your duty, for how else will your sons learn but by your example!"

"Say what you wish to me, father, but I will not have you speak to Ellen in this degrading way! We agreed on the wording of our vows. Ellen is her own person, as free as any man."

"You dare to contradict me---when to do so is to contradict the very words of the Bible!"

"This little talk is a bit too late, old man---John has slipped one past you!"

I heard Mrs. Flagg gasp as John and I turned toward the voice behind us---my father's voice!

"What are you doing in my home---how dare you walk in uninvited?" Reverend Flagg was spluttering indignantly.

I could only stand rooted to the floor---afraid to think of what had brought him here.

"I knocked, but you were making too much noise to hear---and your captive audience was spellbound, so I came on in."

I heard the ice in his voice. I knew what was about to happen, and that I could do nothing to stop it!

"Got yourself quite a man, didn't you, Ellen! At least he tried to defend you---I hear that's about all he'll be able to do for you!" He turned to face John. "Any truth in that? And I don't think I have to spell it out any plainer!"

I looked at John, his face was ashen as he returned father's stare. His voice was empty of any emotion when he answered.

"It's true."

"You must be crazy! What were you going to tell Ellen---a girl wants a family! Well, she won't have to live with this, I've got lawyers, damn good ones! You'll be hearing from them!"

"No---father---wait! You're wrong, all wrong---" I was all but screaming at him. But he swung on his heel and stalked out, ignoring me.

"Let him go, Ellen."

"John, I don't know how he knew, I told no one, I wouldn't ever---"

"I know that." With his arm about my waist, he turned me to face his parents. Mrs. Flagg sat like a statue, pale and unseeing as she stared at the empty doorway.

"I demand an explanation! Of what is Thomas Jordane accusing you?"

I watched John, impaled on the steel gaze of Reverend Flagg, and in that moment, I saw him give up trying to be all his father wanted of him.

"Father---Ellen and I will not have the children you expect."

"What!" Reverend Flagg squawked, sounding as much like a crow as I'd always thought he looked. "Ellen is barren---you knew this and yet you married her?"

"Listen to me, Father, and you, Mother, ---" included for the first time, Mrs. Flagg watched John with a look of half hope and half dread that filled me with pity. "---there will be no children simply because there will be no union---the fault is with me, not Ellen. I'm sorry you had to find this out, today of all days and in this way---"

I knew John's last words were wasted on his father. The old man's face went paste-white, then as black-red as raw liver.

"You! You've caused this---" Flinging back the cover, he was on his feet, shaking his fist at his wife, leaning over her chair as his thin body trembled visibly. "You've caused this with your pampering of him---your selfish demands on me and your complaints! How could I set a proper example with you undermining me at every turn! You've been the devil's partner, not mine! And see what it's gotten you!" He pointed a bony finger at John.

Mrs. Flagg's voice snaked out like a whip cracking in the air as John and I stood frozen. "Shut up! You are never to speak like that of John again! He is more of a man than you've ever been---do you hear me---John is a far better son than you deserve!"

I was sure it was the first time Mrs. Flagg had openly defied her husband, for he seemed suddenly to shrink, stepping backward toward the bed with his hands in front of his face as if to ward off her stinging words.

"The devil is in you, both of you---he's trying to get at me through the two of you---" gasping, he fell back onto the bed, feebly brushing at John's hands as he hurried to lift his father into a more comfortable position. "Where is Rachel, I want her here---"

At a nod from John, I hurried from the room. *This is a nightmare*---the words ran over and over in my mind as I ran across the lawn.

In the door of the reception hall I looked around for Rachel. I rushed to her and grabbed her arm.

"Ellen, you look absolutely wild-eyed! What is it, if Rex is back---"

"No, it's you father---he's terribly upset, he's asking for you! John sent me to bring you!"

"Oh for Pete's sake! I told you he'd cry wolf once too often, and this is it! If he isn't really ill, I'll kill him myself!"

"Everybody's been wonderin' where you went---don't seem proper for the bride and groom to go sneakin' off!" Betha's booming voice drew attention to us, blocking a quiet exit.

"Bertha, the Reverend Flagg is ill and wants to see Rachel. Will you make an announcement? Give our apologies and thank everyone for John and me." The irritation in her voice would normally have provoked a sharp retort---but I knew Bertha was pleased with her assignment. She was already puffing importantly off to the front of the room.

I tightened my grip on Rachel's arm. "Come on, there's no time to waste!"

"Ellen, don't be so frantic, this is old stuff, he just can't stand not being the center of attention."

"No---my father was at the house, he knows about

John---now your parents know!"

At that Rachel flew from the room and I followed, certain that the look on Rachel's face promised another battle for her father.

But as we entered the house John met us. "I've already called the doctor. I think he has had at least a mild attack. Try not to upset him further."

It was easy to see Rachel was not overly concerned, but she said nothing and the three of us went into the bedroom.

Mrs. Flagg spoke. "Isaac, Rachel is here, so you may speak to her."

"All of you---come here where I can see you."

John and Rachel stood by their mother. I stayed at the foot of the bed, feeling very much an intruder.

"I called you here for your benefit, not mine---I know I am drying, and this is the last example I can set for you. I have been a good and faithful servant of the Lord and that knowledge gives me all the comfort I need. But I want you here to see how a real Christian dies! A true Christian has no fear of death, he welcomes it, as I do---"

"I think the doctor is here. I'll let him in." Rachel paused beside me. "See Ellen, what did I tell you?"

I'd been too intent on the scene before me to hear the doctor arrive. But Rachel was back immediately with a quiet-voiced, heavy set man at her side.

"Isaac, I told you not to overdo at John's wedding, you should have listened." As he talked he motioned us out, only Mrs. Flagg remained inside.

The three of us stood just outside the closed door. I knew Rachel wanted to ask questions, but she read the agonized look in John's eyes and wisely refrained.

"Can you stay here with them tonight, Sis?"

"Sure. Rex wants to see me this evening, but I'll work something out."

"Rex is back? I didn't know." A look passed over John's face that made me shiver. "You're the one, aren't you, Rachel---you told Rex all that I trusted you to keep secret--- and he told Ellen's father!"

Just then the doctor came out. "You may go in, but don't excite him. This time it's real. I'm calling an ambulance."

As we went in, we heard Mrs. Flagg speaking patiently but without feeling. "Now, Isaac, you must go---you need things that can't be done here. I'll go with you."

"No! All of you---get out! I'm not going!"

John spoke. "We'd better wait in the living room; he can't be upset."

"Opal, where are you going?" There was no fire and brimstone in his voice now, and we stood at the door looking back at him, surprised at the sudden change.

"You said you didn't need us. We're leaving you alone as you requested." Mrs. Flagg answered in a detached tone.

"I'm afraid---I don't want to be alone---Opal---stay with me!"

We stood, each as uncertain as the other. "Opal---I need you---the devil wants me---he's here in this room!" Reverend Flagg's voice was shrill with fear. "I won't stay in here alone!" He pushed the cover away and was on his feet---one wavering step, then another---"Opal---I'm afraid to die---" he staggered. John lunged forward but was not in time and the old Reverend crumpled to the floor.

I ran, called for the doctor. "Something has happened, he's fallen!"

The doctor rushed past and I went on to the kitchen. I knew Reverend Flagg was not crying wolf now, I was sure he was dying.

*My father has caused this---the Reverend's death will be his fault---and what he's done to John is even worse---*I stood, staring outside, trying not to imagine what was happening in the bedroom.

"Ellen---"

I turned. "John! Here, sit down---" I could see he was unaware of my words, even of my touch as I pressed him toward a chair. "Is he---" I couldn't finish my question, for I saw in John's eyes a hurt deeper than one heart was meant to bear.

"It was a lie---everything he ever told me---even with

us there he was alone---he died alone---he begged mother to hold him and she couldn't bring herself to touch him---he cried for God and thought God couldn't hear him---"

"Oh, John, I'm so sorry---my father did this, he caused it all!"

"It's my fault, Ellen, what I am and what I've done has killed my father!"

His tortured expression frightened me. "John, you need someone---I'll call Reverend Stewart---"

"No, Ellen, I know what I have to do."

"John, where are you going---let me come with you---" he shut the door on my words.

"Where's John? Mom wants him to---"

"Rachel, he's leaving and I don't think he should be alone, he's too upset---I'll be back---" I ran outside. I was too late to see in which direction John had driven, but I was sure I knew.

My car was parked in back of the church. The keys---I slipped into the small room where I'd changed into my wedding dress. I grabbed up my purse, digging for the keys.

Pressing for all the speed I dared, I headed for Fox Hollow. But as I pulled up at the house, John's car was not in sight. My heart sank. I ran to the front door and went in. As I stood wondering where to look for father, he came into the hall.

"Ellen! I was hoping you'd have the sense to walk out! It'll be all right; I'll get you out of this mess!" He took my arm and steered me into the study. "We can talk in here, no use letting anymore of this get round. We've got plans to make---"

"Will you shut up and listen for once!"

An angry flush started to flame up from his open collar into his face. The telephone rang, stalling his reply. "This is the call I've been waiting for---I want complete privacy!"

I shrugged. It was useless. Out in the hall I could hear Bertha in the kitchen, whistling as she started the evening meal.

"I'd like a cup of coffee, Bertha."

Her jaw dropped at my entrance. "My stars! If it ain't the bride---ain't this a bit unusual? Where's your husband?"

I poured my coffee and sat down at the table. "Was John here---just a while ago?"

Bertha's eyes lit with greedy interest. "I sure ain't seen him---don't you know where your man is?"

"Reverend Flagg is dead. John is taking it badly."

"The old Reverend---dead?" Bertha plopped onto a chair. "Well, I swan!"

"Bertha, was Rex Post here today to see my father?"

"Ersey told me Rex was here---I was still at the reception, but Ersey said Rex was all fit to be tied, hoppin' mad at Thomas over somethin'. Then Thomas went flyin' off up the drive---" she broke off and stared at me. "So that's where he went, to see John and the old Reverend---the cats out of the bag now, ain't it!"

"You know?"

"Sure I know! Ain't I always told you I know everythin' worth knowin' around these parts---pays off, too! I wasn't a bit happy with you bein' back here, but when I seen who you was gonna marry I didn't mind near so much---wouldn't be no grandsons for Thomas!"

"How could you have known---no one else did, except Rachel, and Rex---"

"Me and Rex got a business deal---always have had---I pay him plenty for good information! Don't matter if you know now that you're married to John and out of my way!"

"So that's how you knew about our plans to sabotage that fox hunt years ago!"

"Yep! Rex sold you out! Cost me twenty dollars, but it sure was a bargain---course Rex's price has gone up considerable since then!"

"Would it surprise you to know why Rex was so angry when he found out I was being married today?"

"Oh, I always knowed Rex wanted to marry you to get his hands on Fox Hollow---I never trusted him, I just used him! I knew Thomas was pushin' you at Rex since you been back, but you're too stubborn to do what Thomas wants---besides you think you're too good for Rex---don't ask me why!"

"So you think you've got everything under control?"

"Just about---and ain't nothin' gonna stop me now!"

"Well, if you can pull it off, you're welcome to it!"

"You sayin' you know I'm tryin' to get my land back and you ain't gonna try to interfere?"

"If I intended to stop you, I wouldn't have married John, would I?"

"I guess you wouldn't, at that!"

To my surprise she refilled my coffee cup, a gesture of truce I assumed.

"I'll have some of that coffee, Bertha." My father came in. The anger I'd stirred was gone, there was an undercurrent of excitement about him now. "That call was from Megan---she'll be here tomorrow!" Bertha and I both stared as he spoke with a broad smile.

"Here? "Bertha asked flatly.

"Yes, here." He turned to face me. "I'll have you both here again!"

I heard Bertha slam the coffee pot down on the stove as I stood up. "I won't be here; I have my own place---John and I will be there. Why is Megan coming now?"

"Ellen, of course you'll be here---you can't live with John! He's made a fool of me---and you! I called Megan after Rex told me the facts and explained it all to her---I don't know why she didn't come for your wedding, but she's coming now. She knows you need her, I made sure of that."

"How dare you tell Megan! I already knew about John---he told me---I married him so you'd leave me alone---you forced me into it!"

"You knew you were marrying a man who couldn't give you children---you did this on purpose? What kind of a trick were you pulling?"

"John and I married to gain some peace from you and from his father---"

"I thought you'd made the choice to stay here---you and John, to raise your sons here---" he was too wrapped up in his own anger to hear anything I said, yet I could hear the bewilderment in his voice. I knew he still could not see what had driven me to this."---so you think you can put one over on me this easily---well, that's too bad---you've made a big mistake! Go back to John and stay there! You're not to set foot on my land again---you are no longer my daughter! Bertha, you are a witness to this---I am disowning Ellen, she will get nothing from me, since that's what she wants!"

I turned away from him and faced the triumphant expression Bertha could not hold back. "Bertha, I'll leave it to you to tell him what he's caused today---and when Megan knows about it she won't come near Fox Hollow!"

"Wait---what is this---"

But I started out the kitchen door, and as it closed behind me Bertha's eager voice was already gaining momentum.

When I turned my car into the Flagg drive, Rachel ran to meet me. "Did you find John?"

"No. I hoped he'd come back here. Do you think he went to find Rex?"

"I called Rex, he hasn't seen John. Oh, Ellen, John will never forgive me for telling Rex!"

I didn't know what to say to ease Rachel's pain. "How is your mother?"

"She's resting, the doctor gave her a sedative. It's John she's upset about. Do you want to see her?"

"I just can't, not yet. I couldn't make her feel any better."

"You're probably right. If you'd like to change, your things are still at the church."

I'd forgotten I still wore my wedding dress. "I won't take time. If John tries to reach me at my---our---house in town, I want to be there. Did you see Sam, my gift from John?"

"Yes, but I'm afraid I laughed---John was insulted! He was sure you'd love the dog---do you?"

"I think Sam is a lovely gift---help me get her out to the car. I see John was thorough, he bought dogfood and everything!"

As I drove away, I saw Rachel in my rear-view mirror, looking unhappy and alone. *And what are you?* I ignored my question and with one hand rubbed Sam's cropped ears. The big dog seemed glad of my company---as I was of hers.

John was not at the house. I followed Sam as she poked through the rooms. Her curiosity satisfied, she stood staring at me as if she expected something.

"Hungry, Sam?" I put out food and water. Sam's appetite was equal to her size.

It was deep dusk now, and there was nothing I could do but wait. I knew no one to call, Rachel knew John's habits much better than I, if there was anything to be done she would do it.

But where is he? Had he simply kept on driving, running from the havoc caused by Rex and my father---or had Rex lied when he told Rachel he had not seen John---if John confronted Rex disaster could be the only result!

And there was Megan---coming at the request of my father. He had told her about John and me. Had he told her I knew now that she was not my aunt, but my mother? I could still call her and tell her not to come---no, let her come! I was through bending backward to avoid trouble, through with side-stepping facts, no matter how painful they might be!

"Sam, there is going to be a terrible explosion---but when the dust settles only the truth will be standing, surely that will be better for us all!"

Sam followed me about as I changed into comfortable clothes, then I took her out to explore the yard staying near the raised windows in case the telephone rang.

Later, I stretched out on the sofa, drained of all energy. Sam sprawled on the rug nearby. Much later the telephone woke us both. I jerked up, disoriented as to time and place.

"Hello?"

"Ellen, it's Rachel---I've found John."

Nine

Three days later the church was again filled beyond its capacity. I could feel the eyes pricking my back and if I met a gaze it would fill with tearful compassion---the new bride had not been accepted with good grace but as a new widow I had been clutched to every female bosom and smothered with sympathy. I could plainly see their relief that it was me---not themselves, or their daughter, or their sister, sitting in the front pew.

"---and there he was, married just a few hours---but nothing would do but he go and help someone who needed him! Never did hear who it was that called for him---if it were me, I wouldn't want it known either! Oh, that young Reverend was a saint---a saint! And his poor bride---" at that point the whisperers dissolved into tears. I'd overheard several versions of the story repeated in hushed tones.

Rachel had not exactly told people it had happened that way, but she had helped their assumption along with a nod and a word at the right times.

"---and to think---while your dear brother (or husband or son, depending on whether Rachel, myself, or Mrs. Flagg was the captive listener) was on his way to do a good deed---his own father was dying---" and the tears would start again.

The story suited everyone. There was no question in anyone's mind but what John had simply misjudged his speed on the hairpin curves and his car had plunged into the ravine, crashing through the trees.

But had it been an accident? I knew John was distraught---had it already happened when I drove past on my way into town? If I'd been more alert, I might have seen John's car in the ravine---I could have gotten help---he might have lived! Had John wanted to live? ---I knew Rachel had the same question in her mind, I could see it torturing her.

A chill ran through me despite the fact that the small sanctuary was much too warm. The church depended on ceiling fans and open windows to cool it, but the air was thick and unmoving, heavy with moisture soon to be released. It held close, and still the sticky-sweet fragrance from what seemed hundreds of flowers banked about the two caskets.

Poor old Reverend Flagg. He had so wanted to always be the center of attention. Now, even in his death he was eclipsed by John. As if he knew this, his features were set in a condemning expression of disapproval.

I glanced at Mrs. Flagg. It was John she mourned, and I suspected everyone knew it. She was clinging to Rachel, her eyes shut against the sight before her.

It was time to start; if more people came, they would have to remain outside. I turned and looked around. Folding chairs filled the outside aisles and none were empty.

There was Bertha and Ersey---Bertha with her face all screwed up and her eyes clamped shut. A woeful shake of her head and the tear or two that she'd managed to conjure up would seep out. I knew it was a supreme effort for her to pretend the same spontaneous feelings of her fellow churchwomen and her pretense disgusted me. Then I saw Rex Post. He'd been watching me and grinned when he caught my eye. I jerked back around.

Reverend Stewart, John's friend, was conducting the service. As the music stopped, he took his place. Megan gave my hand a pat of encouragement. I thought how shocked people would be if they knew what Megan knew, that my grief was that for a lost friend---not a lost love.

Directly behind me was my father, himself in an awkward position of his own making. Having disowned me in front of Bertha, who I was certain had spread that juicy tidbit far and wide, he could hardly take his place beside me as a father would be expected to do---even if I would allow it. I knew with Megan here he longed to be in our pew, near her. For Megan had come directly to me upon her arrival, and when I'd told her I was no longer a bride, but a widow---and that I was not now even a daughter to Thomas Jordane---she had been livid with anger at his action.

But I had been thrilled by what she said, and for the hundredth time I took comfort in her words---"I've given Thomas every chance, Ellen, but no more! He's hurt you too often! I've longed to tell you this---I never dreamed it would be amid such circumstances---but Ellen, you are mine---my own daughter---my own little girl that I love, have always loved---"

"Megan, I know." And we'd stood, looking at each other, trying to cross the hurt and the lost time---then those things were pushed aside as we held each other. No words were needed or even possible as for those few moments nothing existed except Megan and me!

And then we had talked, until I had but one question left.

"Was it because of father's threats of a court battle that you let him keep me all those years ago? He seems to think there was some other reason, but he has never been sure of what it could have been."

"How like Thomas not to understand! It was not

because of any threats he made---I left you for such an obvious reason---I thought you were loved and that you were happy, I was convinced of that each time I saw you. You seemed so satisfied---I thought it would be too selfish of me to take you from all that was familiar and meant home to you. When Claudette finally told me how she really felt, that she wanted me to take you, I couldn't get there fast enough. She had fabricated some story to tell Thomas, she was so afraid of his reaction---but I was determined to take you with me in any event. Bertha didn't know that, and in her malicious way she meant to make certain you left Fox hollow with me. So she told Thomas about the hunt sabotage your friends planned, enlarging it to serve her own purpose."

So now I knew it had been out of love that Megan left me---not for the reasons my father said! Everything would be all right between Megan and me. I was clinging to that now.

I realized the last of the people had filed past the caskets. We walked out of the church into a light mist of rain. Under the canopies we were again seated in the front row. People stopped to speak as we waited.

"Megan Jordane---glad you was able to get here---too bad you couldn't come for the weddin'! Then you'd had at least one happy day with Ellen and Reverend John---why wasn't you here, anyhow?" Bertha's question was asked in her usual loud voice, and I saw several people looking interested in her answer, father among them. It was the one question I had not been brave enough to ask.

"It simply was not possible."

I saw Megan's quiet answer did not satisfy Bertha. But seeing it was all Megan intended to say, Bertha moved on.

Reverend Stewart spoke again---then we were led away---back into the rain, heavier now with thunder building on all sides. We moved quickly toward the cars.

"Megan---" We turned. Father walked toward us sheltered by a large umbrella. I could see he was trying to maintain a polite indifference, but his eyes---his eyes sought Megan with such longing that I turned away. "I'll wait in the car."

A funeral attendant held my umbrella and opened the car door, then got in the front seat to wait for Megan. I watched out the side window, fascinated at the sight of the two people who were my parents standing together under the big umbrella. Through the streaming glass their figures blended into the trees, grey with rain. I could only wonder at how different our lives would have been had we lived them together.

At last Megan left him and came to the car. As we pulled away, he still stood looking after her, his solitary figure distorted y the curtain of rain. I glanced at Megan. Something in her face gave me a little jolt of alarm, but I couldn't intrude and we were silent during the ride back into town.

When we were seated in my comfortable living room with a tray of coffee and sandwiches, Megan spoke. "Something is going on at Fox Hollow. Thomas wanted to talk to me earlier, as you saw, but it was not the time or place and he told me only a few brief facts."

I watched Megan as she stirred cream into her coffee. She had changed in the two months since I'd seen her. She was thinner, but it was more than a physical thing. There was a strange determination about her---as if she poured into even the smallest task an unwavering will of iron.

I tried to reassure her. "Megan, please don't be so concerned, we know I'll be excluded from father's will, he probably wanted to explain his reasons to you in full."

"For once, Ellen, it's not Thomas I'm worried about. Bertha is the one who bears watching, she is different now. I know she has never forgiven Ersey for selling Fox Hollow; it was in her family for generations and somehow, they eked out a living. She bitterly resents Ersey for failing to do better. She wants that land back!"

"Everyone knows how Bertha feels, she's never made a secret of it---father always laughed and egged her on---no one takes her seriously---what can she really do?"

"You're right, no one takes Bertha seriously---and that's a mistake. Now I can see she has had a plan all these years, and she has worked at it so methodically and so consistently that no one has noticed---now she thinks success is within her reach!"

I stared at Megan. In one cold flash the past met the present and I knew. Bertha was the one who killed Nolan. My little brother had posed a more serious threat at that time than even I---she had had time in which to deal with me, there were ways of discrediting me with my father. But Nolan was the true off-spring of Thomas and Claudette---the real barrier to Bertha's plan, and she had eliminated him as soon as it could be done in a way that I could be blamed. And she had built on that firm foundation at every turn.

Megan continued. 'Thomas is playing right into Bertha's hands, I'm sure of it! She's a dangerous woman---I tried to tell him, but he shrugged it off."

"Why would he believe it? He still thinks I caused Nolan's death---but I know it was Bertha---father doesn't know what she is really capable of doing!"

Megan came to sit beside me on the sofa, taking my hand. "Ellen, stay away from Bertha. She won't consider you a threat now. Frankly, I'm relieved Thomas is taking you out of his will, he has insured your safety."

"You're right, but I just can't stand to think of Bertha getting away with---with murder! And I think she has!"

"Don't try to prove anything, you couldn't after all this time. And you'd be placing yourself in danger. I know you didn't let Nolan fall down those stairs---your account of that day is very different from the story Bertha told---but she'll trip herself up somehow---sometime!"

Megan was so upset that now I held her hand. "You're right, I know you are. We can only wait for the truth to come out. In the meantime, I have the new shop---and I have my mother---I'm very happy with both---I'm very fortunate!"

She smiled and relaxed, leaning her head back against the sofa and closing her eyes. I studied her. Megan was as striking as ever, her tanned face was framed by her chestnut hair still in the smooth chignon she'd worn under a wide brimmed black straw hat earlier. She still wore the beige silk dress trimmed with black and rust stitching. Now she looked at me, her hazel eyes clear and warm.

"So many mistakes, Ellen---but we've managed to find each other in spite of them. I feel very lucky, too. But I'm afraid I have to go back to Wilmington tomorrow. I have a very important appointment I can't reschedule."

"So soon---I hoped you could stay awhile!" I didn't want her to go---I wanted time for us to be mother and daughter instead of aunt and niece.

"I know, Ellen, I am sorry. But later, soon I hope, we can plan some time to ourselves. Unless I can pour you another cup of coffee, I think I'll have a relaxing bath and go to bed; my flight out isn't early but I am tired."

We'd both be better off to go to bed and put this day behind us, I thought. "I've had enough coffee. Run your tub, I'll clear these things away."

The rain had stopped some while ago, but it was a grey evening that would turn into darkness earlier than usual. I had changed from the tan and cream striped dress I'd worn to the funeral into slacks, a cool shirt and sandals. I stepped out the kitchen door into the breezeway. Sam trotted up to me, wanting company. I sat down on the concrete step and she settled at my feet. I was already very attached to my new pet, Sam showed every sign of being a good watch dog. She instinctively placed herself between me and anyone she had not met before. Megan had said Sam was a comforting presence. Megan---what had father told her when they stood under the umbrella after the service---as always, Megan's opinion still mattered to him.

I kicked my sandals off and walked over the wet grass, feeling restless and lonely. I didn't want Megan to leave tomorrow---I didn't want Mitch to be in Philadelphia with Denise---and there was Bertha---guilty of little Nolan's death---I was sure of it! But what could I do---*surely something, after Megan leaves, I'll think of something!*

I heard Sam's low, insistent growls and I tried to see through the dusk. I had not noticed the big dog leaving my side. I had not bothered to turn on any outside lights when I came out and now it was just dark enough to make me unsure.

Sam growled again and I realized she was in the side yard. As quickly as I could manage, I went through the breezeway and around the house. The light at the end of the driveway turned on automatically at dusk and in its glow, I saw Bertha standing just inside the yard. Sam was between her and the house and I knew Bertha was afraid to move in any direction.

Not wanting Bertha to call out and attract Megan's attention, I hurried toward the statue-still pair.

"Call this crazy dog off---you out of your mind, keepin' a dangerous animal like this? Everyone knows Dobermans are killers!"

"Hardly, Bertha, Sam's a watchdog, that's all---here girl. Now, what do you want?"

"Well, can't we go in and sit? Ain't too friendly feelin' out here. I'd like to see Megan, too."

"It would feel no friendlier inside, and I don't want to disturb Megan."

"Ain't you just as uppidy as ever! Well, people don't change overnight, I guess. You're gonna need a little time to get used to not bein' Thomas Jordane's daughter---legal anyhow, and that's what counts!"

"That hardly concerns you, Bertha."

"I just came to say I been sort of harsh with you in the past, Ellen, now I'm sorry about that. No need of us havin' hard feelin's 'tween us anymore."

I felt hot words boiling in my throat and I could barely make the effort of choking them back. This woman was a murderess, I knew it and couldn't prove it---not yet!

"I can see you're all upset---got a right to be, now you're a widow and all that. Well, you're young, you'll get over it, ain't like you was really grievin', seein' why you married John. Maybe you'll decide to go back to North Carolina, seems a change would be better than stayin' where there's so many sad reminders! I just stopped by to clear the air, so I'll be goin'---uh, I wondered if Megan is stayin' on awhile or goin' right back?"

"She's leaving tomorrow"

Bertha nodded. "That's good." She went out the gate

and got into Ersey's pickup. I watched her drive away. What had she really come for---what would she have said if I'd allowed her to see Megan?   But Megan was right about Bertha being different, she was in a hurry about something---but what, why this sudden, intense determination I sensed in her?

I took Sam inside.   John had said she'd be good protection, and she was.   But now I'd no longer need protection from Rex, I was going to be disinherited, he could no longer get Fox Hollow through me.   Megan had said father had done me a favor, but while I was safe from Rex, and even Bertha, that meant father would be the one standing between Bertha and the land she wanted so badly.

I shivered---suddenly sure I knew what Bertha intended to do, but I also knew no one would believe me. My father least of all!

Ten

Sleep was out of the question. I was too keyed-up---angry---frightened---I longed desperately to talk to someone---Bertha's unexpected visit had left me badly shaken. Bertha Hunter---just an outspoken, rough-as-a-cob-but-with--heart-of-gold-country-woman! That was the image she had sought to build and hide behind, one that allowed her to scheme and connive, even kill, I was certain, while seeming to be an innocent victim herself! For Bertha had created the impression it was through Ersey's mismanagement and lack of ambition she had lost her homeplace, what she called her birthright and what was now Fox Hollow.

She had talked about it so much that no one paid her any real attention, father listened only if he was in the mood to antagonize her. As on one occasion when I'd walked into the big kitchen at Fox Hollow to hear father saying, "Now Bertha, Ersey Hunter's a good man---you should give him his due!"

"If he'd worked half as hard for himself as he does for you this land would still be mine! There wouldn't be no Fox Hollow!"

I had been surprised at Bertha's boldness. She had put more spite than usual into her reply, and I knew by the slight narrowing of father's eyes that he would put her in her place. "Ah, but he didn't! Some people are meant to work for others, not every man can be his own boss. Takes a lot of self-discipline. You and Ersey should have raised a family. He'd been more concerned with working your place if he'd had sons to leave it to!"

Bertha had seemed to puff up even larger in her indignation. Wasn't my fault Ersey was firin' blanks--- nothin' I could do 'bout that---wasn't my fault!"

Satisfied at having ruffled Bertha's feathers, father had just chuckled and gone outside. I had quickly followed, knowing that if I stayed behind Bertha would vent her frustration by giving me the most unpleasant tasks she could find.

But that had been years ago, now Bertha seemed to be almost in a panic to make her move---as if she suddenly had a limited amount of time in which to reach her goal---why? I had no answer. Megan and I had gone over everything and resolved nothing. There was no one else I could talk to.

I'd settle for a warm bath, it seemed to have worked for Megan. I'd heard no sound from her room. I was sure she was not aware of Bertha's visit.

When I finally got into bed, Sam came into my room to sprawl out on the rug. And, as so many other times, I was glad of her company.

When I awoke sunshine was spilling across the floor. I sat up. Sam was gone and the door to my room was shut. I grabbed my robe and checked the time. I couldn't believe I'd slept so late!

I found Megan in the kitchen. "Well! About time--- here, I just made coffee. I've been out already, I left a note in case you were up before I returned. Sam is outside."

"What about your flight?"

"There's a plenty of time. Now have your coffee, I'm going to have some with you."

Megan wore a red linen dress simply styled for comfortable traveling. I thought again how lovely she was. I couldn't imagine what a different man my father must once have been for Megan to have loved him---but I knew how foolish he had been to lose her!

"Was there something you needed, Megan, were we out of coffee or cream?"

"No. I called Thomas and asked him to meet me in town, I didn't want anyone, particularly Bertha, to know. We've had a long talk---I decided I couldn't go back to North Carolina until I knew what was going on---and until I'd convinced him of a few facts. Now he knows I believe Bertha caused little Nolan's death and that she encouraged Claudette to ride in the hunt that day when she was obviously not fit to do so---and that she has tried to turn him against you in every possible way!" Megan stopped for breath, looking as ready to do battle as I was sure she had looked when she saw father. "We covered other things too, Ellen, I'm afraid I left nothing unsaid once I started, but I feel worlds better for it!"

"You could say anything to father, Megan, and he'd listen. He loves you still, I know he does---he knows his biggest mistake was in losing you---" I stopped. This was not something I felt I should talk about. After all, I would not be sharing my life with the one I loved either! Mitch had made his choice; he was with Denise.

"Ellen, Thomas is starting to pay for his mistakes, and I think it frightens him. I hope you can understand him better someday. I hope you'll be able to forgive him."

"I know he can't make himself admit his mistakes!"

"He has no choice now but to admit to several! This morning he told me when he bought Bertha's land she insisted on a conditional clause. It states if Thomas does not have an heir named, either his wife or his child, by the time he is fifty, half ownership reverts to Bertha---complete ownership if Thomas should die with no heir named!"

I was stunned. "How could he have agreed?"

"At that time Thomas wanted the land desperately, and he would never have considered it a real possibility that he would not have as many children as he wished!"

"No, he would have felt quite safe in agreeing to such a stipulation! But Bertha once told me whatever was worth knowing around Fox Hollow, she knew it---she probably knew more about Claudette's state of health at that time than father did! She'd made her plans, even then!"

"I think you're right. And Thomas will be fifty in less than four months. I expect Bertha scents victory and Thomas is feeling the pressure---he knows he should have held his temper when you married John, now he has to eat crow, a dish he's never tried before!"

"And poor Claudette---" I spoke without thinking, only now realizing to some small degree the tragic life the woman I'd called mother had lived.

"Yes. Poor Claudette. My involvement with Thomas was before I'd met her, but I soon came to pity her. I know she truly loved Thomas in the beginning."

I stood up, automatically clearing our few dishes away. "We have nothing to go on but our suspicions, we can't prove anything. We have no facts with which to confront Bertha, or to give the authorities!"

"I know, Ellen, and I want you to promise you won't try to force the issue with Bertha."

"It would be useless, Megan, you're right. Now, I hate to say it, but we must get started if we're to have time to stop at the shop." I wondered again what the important appointment could be that Megan was rushing back to keep. But she made no mention of it and I didn't pry.

Rachel had been almost desperate to get back to work. Although the shop had been closed because of John's death, few people realized the connection and Rachel was handling things very well. When Megan and I arrived at the shop Rachel and the woman I'd hired before the re-opening had things well in hand. Rachel had seemed to gain poise and self-confidence since she'd started at Paige Two. She was just as pleased by Megan's approval as I.

"The shop is lovely---I'm proud of it, and of all of you.

I know I'm going to enjoy your progress reports!"

Rachel walked us to the door. "I'd like to stop by and talk awhile after we close, Ellen, if you'll be home."

I told Rachel when I expected to be back, then Megan and I got in my car and headed out of town toward Indianapolis.

When we reached Weir Cook airport there was still time before Megan's flight and I suggested lunch. I was not hungry, really, but I wanted something to help occupy my attention.

We nibbled and talked about Megan's painting and the perfect weather for her flight---it was a day as opposite from yesterday as could possibly be. But I wanted her not to go---I only knew I didn't want us to be apart---

"That's my flight they're announcing, Ellen---I'm truly sorry to be leaving so soon---now you must be careful---and stay away from Bertha!"

I was startled by the forcefulness of her words. "Of course I'll be careful, Megan, now you must promise you won't worry so!"

She laughed a little. "All right---I'm just being an over-protective mother! Remember, I haven't had you as a daughter very long!"

"It's---special to me, Megan, being your daughter." I wished I could bring myself to call her mother, and right now I felt she wished it, too. But just her very name held more meaning for me. Megan was the dearer of the two words, I hoped she knew that.

We hugged goodbye and she left promptly. I felt my smile wobble as she turned for a last wave. She looked near tears herself. But we'd be together soon, I was sure.

I left the terminal and found my car. Then I was threading my way through the traffic out onto the city by-pass. An hour or so later I pulled up at the Birkdale's house.

The small car Rachel drove was at the curb. The car was the first major purchase she had ever made totally on her own and she was proud of it.

As I walked through the breezeway, I saw Rachel in the back yard tossing a stick for Sam. Sam was watching her performance with an air of disdain.

"That's very good, Rachel!" I called out. Sam came loping over to me.

Rachel laughed. "This dog of yours knows no tricks at all!"

"Give her time, she will! Come on in, I'm tired and I know you must be."

Sam trailed us into the living room and we all found comfortable places.

"You hated to see Megan go, I know. When you told me your true relationship, I couldn't believe it! When we were kids and you talked about your Aunt Megan, I always thought you were exaggerating, until the day I finally met her. But she was just as you said, beautiful---and so nice to me and John---it was the day your---Claudette---was injured. I think it's wonderful, Megan being your mother, I wish you'd always known."

"Yes, so do I. But what about you, Rachel, are you sure we haven't reopened too soon---I don't want you to push too hard."

"I need to keep as busy as possible. And mom is already making plans to go to her sister's next week. She needs the change; she can't stay here." Rachel started drumming her fingers on the chair arm, looking miserable.

"I've found out some things, Ellen. Rex came by my apartment last night. He'd been drinking just enough to loosen his tongue. He swore he didn't see John the day of the accident. John was headed to see Rex, I'm sure, but he never arrived."

"And you think Rex was telling the truth?"

"Yes, I do. But there's more---we had a terrible argument---I was furious Rex had told your father the personal things about John I'd been so foolish as to confide to him. Rex lost his temper with me so completely that he told me everything. Now I see all that John was trying to protect you from."

"Rachel, I'm sorry---"

"No, Ellen, I'm over Rex! I can see now he used me, how be influenced me---I'm ashamed I ever thought I needed him for anything! This job has made me realize I can count on myself. I'm not the lost cause dad made me out to be---I wish I could prove that to John!"

"He always knew it, Rachel, he was waiting for you to prove it to yourself."

"Well, I know it now, and you've helped me see it. Now I can help you, I hope---between the two of us we can decide the best thing to do. You see, Rex told me he had intended to bulldoze you into marriage, any way he could---he thought he'd succeed, his ego is too big to consider failure and he had your father's approval. But now he knows you are to be disinherited---Bertha loved telling that around---Rex's big plans will go up in smoke unless he can interest Bertha in his scheme."

"What is Rex planning?"

"Rex never intended to continue with the hunts as your father assumed, he would do. He intends to combine Fox Hollow with his own smaller property and design an exclusive housing development with a golf course and country club---it would make Rex a very rich man. He's already working on getting the backing---some real estate broker out of Indianapolis is ready to help---Bertha will probably agree with Rex, she'll know there's much more money to be made going that direction. There is enough land with Fox Hollow to do it without Rex's property, but Rex can get the backing and he knows how to set it up, so Bertha needs Rex, and Rex needs Bertha's co-operation."

I stared at Rachel, trying to sort out all she'd told me. "I may be safe as long as I'm out of the will, but my father isn't"

Rachel stood, then moved about the room. "Speaking of being safe, Rex said something strange. Bertha told him you'd had a threatening note and 'phone call---telling you to leave while you could. She asked him if he knew anything about it, but he doesn't---if neither of them was responsible, who could it be? And why didn't you tell me about it?"

"I admit I thought Bertha was the one. Now I don't have a clue as to who it was---but there's been nothing since the shop opened, I think it's all over. I didn't mention it to you because frankly, I felt rather foolish not to even know who my enemy was! They even called me Foxey-Locksey! Remember how I hated that nickname?"

"Yes, I remember---I hope you're right about it being over. Think about what I've told you and we can decide what to do about it---if you want to tell your father or not---I promised mom I'd take her to dinner, so I'd better go. That empty house gives her the creeps!"

I followed Rachel to the door. "I'm coming in to the shop tomorrow, we'll talk about this when I've had time to sort it out. Thanks for coming by."

Rachel turned. "Oh, Ellen, I almost forgot. Remember the day Denise Graham stopped by the shop with Mitch? Well, it's no wonder she was less than charming to you---Rex was behind even that!"

"I don't see how---"

"Rex wanted Mitch out of the picture, he knew Thomas liked Mitch and would prefer him as a son-in-law, and in case you felt the same way Rex told Denise you were back here to 'latch on to Mitch' as he put it, and that she'd better make her move fast!"

"Denise put herself to a lot of unnecessary effort! Mitch has no interest in me."

"Mitch is back, I saw him today."

I managed to keep my expression non-committal. I even kept from asking if Denise was with him.

With a wave Rachel hurried to her car. I went into the kitchen and stood staring out the window. In the past hour everything had changed---I knew I was safe from further trouble with Rex, but I had to tell father what Bertha and Rex were planning---Fox Hollow, chopped into parcels for building lots---trees uprooted---even entire woods destroyed! I couldn't bear the thought! And it wouldn't happen---somehow, I'd see to that!

And Mitch is back! Is he here to stay---is he alone? Whatever the answers, it would not change anything for me. I doubted if Mitch would understand why I'd married John, a man I didn't love---he'd think I was just as calculating as my father! I had made mistakes, in that area I was my father's daughter, disinherited or not!

"Come on outside, Sam, thinking about all this will drive me mad---let's work on those tricks, we'll show Rachel!"

I needed a diversion and Sam was willing to provide it. She raced for the stick I threw, but growled with mock ferocity when I tried to talk her into giving it up. But I found she was a natural at chase, even giving me a head start before she charged after me.

I was laughing and trying to block her attack when the tone of Sam's growls deepened and the short hair bristled along her back.

"Hello, Ellen."

I turned. "Mitch!" I stared, unable to think of a thing to say as he walked across the yard to me. My mind was wondering what had brought him here while my heart was foolishly content with his presence!"

"I hope you're a little glad to see me."

I managed to drag my eyes away. "I think I'd better introduce you to Sam so she'll quit growling."

Mitch extended his hand and Sam approached to sniff it, at once she was wagging her stumped tail and wriggling with pleasure as Mitch rubbed her ears. "Quite a dog! When did you get her?"

"Sam was a gift from John. I'll tell you about her sometime."

"Ellen, I'm sorry about John. I've just talked to Thomas and he told me what happened, he sees now that he pushed you into that marriage---and that he caused your problem with Rex. He said Megan made him see a lot of things differently."

"What's he doing? Discussing me like he would a sick horse? That man can make me feel so foolish---" I walked away from Mitch to hide the hot rush of angry tears. My pride was tattered enough, if I cried it would have to wait until I was alone---I would not give in to tears now!

"Ellen, don't hide from me---don't make me feel I mean so little to you." He caught up to me. "So much of what's happened to you is my fault. The night of the party I wanted to tell you, warn you really, about the way Thomas was trying to set people up---I just didn't realize he was so serious---then it seemed as if you knew what to expect from him and I had some things to settle of my own before I could be as open as I wanted with you---"

"And where is Denise---or haven't you settled things yet?" There. I had asked.

"That's settled. She's in Philadelphia and I'm here---and that's the only way it can be. When I told Denise how I felt, she told me Rex had warned her about you---then I knew I had to get back, between Rex and Thomas you'd be in for a rough time. I was too late."

"Do you really understand about John and me---or do you think I also manipulate people?"

"You're nothing like that." Now he drew me gently into his arms and I leaned willingly against him, wanting never to leave this safe, warm circle. "Thomas sees what he caused, he said Megan really raked him over the coals. He's different now, I can't explain it, but you'll see what I mean. He wants you to come to Fox Hollow tonight, he wants to talk to you."

"Oh, he does!" I stepped away. "And what would I be letting myself in for this time---he's already disowned me!" I stuffed my shaking hands into my pockets. I was angry and hurt. *What did you think---that Mitch came for reasons of his own?*

Mitch put his hands on my shoulders and turned me to face him. "Thomas didn't think you'd even talk to him if he called you, so he wanted me to ask you---come with me now---" Mitch was talking fast. I thought he was wondering how long I'd listen to him---I was wondering myself! "---Ellen, its important, more so than I'm free to say!"

I stepped out of his hold. "So far you've given me no reason why I should go. I've hardly forgotten that twice he's told me to stay away from Fox Hollow. I'd be a fool to give him the chance to tell me again!"

"Ellen, I understand how you feel, and whether you believe it or not, so does Thomas, now. But there is so much you don't know, and I can't tell you---"

"Then forget it, Mitch! I've had enough secrets! I'm not interested in hearing anymore father may be ready to confess!" I could see Mitch was searching for leverage, a way to change my mind. I shook my head. "There's nothing you can say. Father will have to come to me himself---not through a go-between!"

Something flared in Mitch's eyes---anger, I supposed. But I was angry too, and it was time to get this over. "I'm sure you're doing what you think is right, Mitch, and I appreciate your concern."

I forced myself to return his gaze. His tanned, rather squared face was set with a weariness that stirred the vary feelings I had to forget.

He bent to kiss my cheek. "I'll talk to you again soon, Ellen, and when I do, I won't allow you to dismiss me so easily!"

I watched him go, fighting the urge to call him back. "Pride makes for poor company, Sam---but at least I've got you!" As if she sensed my mood Sam followed me from room to room as I locked the house for the night. It was early, but I was exhausted and sleep would bring tomorrow more quickly. I was eager to get back to the shop, work would be a welcome release.

I was dressed and drinking coffee when the first streaks of gold and rose colored the sky. I felt a strong sense of relief and renewed purpose. I'd put in a full day's work at the shop, then I'd swallow my pride and drive out to Fox Hollow and talk to father. I had to tell him what was going on---once he knew what Rex was planning he could take some action.

Shop hours were nine thirty to five, but it was only eight o'clock when I let myself in the back door. I'd have some quiet time to catch up my bookwork.

I'd worked steadily for some time before I stopped and walked out to the front of the shop. It looked just as I'd envisioned, the neutral shades were an inviting backdrop for the fall fashions that were already arriving in the way the garment industry has of thrusting season upon season.

Sharp tapping on the window startled me and I

hurried to look out. "Come in." I opened the door then re-locked it and stood waiting.

"This is a classy set-up, Ellen. Megan told me you'd done a great job with it."

"Thank you." I'd seldom seen my father away from Fox Hollow and here his sheer masculinity was in direct variance with our surroundings. Megan had once told me he had been very magnetic as a young man---I had no doubt he could still be when he chose.

"Are we alone?"

I nodded. "Let's sit down." I led the way to the office. Father ignored the chairs, moving about in the limited space. He was obviously ill at ease, a feeling I suspected he'd rarely dealt with.

"I tried to reach you at the Birkdale's house. I didn't know you came to work so early."

"I don't always."

"Ellen---" he stood facing me, his hands gripping the back of a chair. I'd never seen him at a loss for words and it gave me a little prick of alarm.

"You're not here to talk about why you sent Mitch to see me last night, or to talk about Fox Hollow, are you?"

"No. I wish I were---I've been played for a fool more ways than one and I'm going to change all that as soon as you're back."

"Back? from where---"

"I'm going against Megan in this, but I think you should know, she's your mother---you should know---" his voice broke and he turned away.

"What are you saying? Megan's all right, isn't she? I just saw her yesterday---answer me!"

"She's ill, she's known for a long time---she told me yesterday morning---made me promise I'd tell you only when I knew things were bad---her doctor called---Megan's been hospitalized."

Everything in the room seemed to shrink except his words. I heard Rachel call a hello from the front of the shop. Father went out to meet her.

I stood up. I had to move---to get to Megan! They

came in. Rachel's stricken look told me she knew.

"I'll sign the necessary checks, Rachel, I don't know how long I'll be away. Just close the shop if it's too much for you." I made my few preparations amid Rachel's murmured assurances that I was not to worry about the shop. Then I walked out with father beside me.

"I've already arranged for a private plane, it's waiting. Do you want to pack a bag?"

"No. Some of my things are still at Megan's house in Wilmington, there's no time anyway. But Sam---my dog---"

"I'll take care of your dog, it can stay in the kennels, Ersey will see to it."

I wasn't pleased at the idea of Sam being in a kennel, but there was no choice. We were headed toward the county airport now.

"Aren't you coming to Wilmington with me?"

"No. It's you Megan loves and needs. I wasn't there when she did need me, now I'd be intruding." He said it without anger, just acceptance. Mitch had been right last night, father was different. "They will be expecting you at the hospital, they've told Megan you're on your way."

"Thank you---" It was all I could manage.

"Ellen---she'll wait for you---I know it!" He stopped the car and we half ran toward the twin engine plane warming up.

Father gathered me to him in a quick, bruising hug that took me totally by surprise, then gave me a hand up into the plane. In the next second we were airborne.

"Might as well try to relax, you've been leaning forward like that since we took off---it won't get us there any sooner. It won't be long; we'll be in Wilmington shortly."

I took the pilot's advice as much as was possible, but my thoughts were speeding on ahead of the small aircraft to Megan. For now I could only wait, and hope, and pray---

The pilot's voice making contact with the Wilmington tower made my heart start pounding again. In a blur of time that seemed to take forever yet was only minutes, I was in a taxi heading for New Hanover Hospital.

I was glad to be alone in the elevator, my knees were

rubbery and I leaned against the wall---it all seemed so unreal!

At the nurses' station I explained who I was. "May I speak with my mother's doctor?"

The nurse nodded, sending an aide off at a brisk pace. In only a moment a man appeared. My eyes were pinned on the slightly built figure with salt and pepper hair, his hand extending to me already though he was still several paces away.

"Miss Jordane---Ellen, if I may, I feel I know you very well. Your mother has talked so much about you these past months."

"Months? Megan's been ill all this time and didn't tell me---why?"

"It was her decision. She wanted it this way, as she said, for her own selfish reasons---although I know there was nothing selfish about them. She just wanted life to stay as normal as possible for you, and herself---we can't blame her for that, can we?"

I shook my head. "Tell me what it is before I go in to her."

"Megan has myelocytic leukemia. She wanted to spare you---she knew time was catching up. She was having a bad time when you married---yes, I know about that--- Megan was very upset at being unable to attend your wedding. Then she rallied and was well enough to travel to Indiana to be with you when your husband was killed. That's the nature of this disease---"

A thousand thoughts and pictures flashed through my mind---Megan, so tired, yet pushing hard to finish her paintings, urging me to set things straight with father, worrying about my spiritual well-being---she wanted all the loose ends gathered up!

"Please, Ellen, for Megan's sake don't cry now---she is being very brave, we can't be any less for her."

"I'm sorry, I didn't know I was crying!" My voice sounded as lost as I felt. I was going to lose Megan! Loneliness was already creeping into my very bones. I searched for a tissue, then repaired the make-up of the strange, tight face reflected in the mirror of my compact.

"That's better. I know how impossible this is for you. You should go in now."

I looked at him. His eyes were incredibly sad. But I was glad to see Megan was more than a patient to him, she was a dear friend as well.

A nurse stepped out of Megan's room as I opened the door, but I was barely aware of her, so caught was I by the sight of Megan lying so still. Her hair seemed the only thing about her with any life as it held the gleam of sunshine coming through the window. This couldn't be happening---not to Megan---not to Megan and me!

I stepped closer. "Megan, I'm here."

Her eyes opened and I was struck by the light they held---so bright, so aware---no one could look like that and be close to death!

"My dear Ellen! I've been waiting for you---everyone told me you were coming---I want to explain---"

I swallowed hard before I could speak. "Megan, there's no need to explain. I understand---I've talked to Doctor Fredon."

"I hope you're not angry at me for keeping another secret from you."

I dropped into a chair near her bed and put my face in my hands. "Megan, I've never been angry with you---I never would be---I love you---

I felt her hand on my hair. "My little girl---you've shown me in a hundred ways, but this is the first time I've heard you say the words---"

Hot tears filled my eyes and my voice was tight with the effort of holding them back as I whispered, "I love you Megan, and I need you here with me---always!" Her lips pressed together in a grimace of pain---I couldn't bear it! "I'll get the nurse---"

"No, Ellen, they've done all they can for me---I can't seem to get my thoughts together---would you pray for me---"

My heart twisted as I took her free hand and began, trusting the words to come.

"Dear Lord, I pray you will ease my mother's pain---I prayed all the long way here that you would not take her from me---now I know she needs you to help her through this time. Give us both the courage to accept your will. I pray for my mother and myself, in Jesus's name. Amen."

Megan's eyes were on me as I raised my head. "Thank you, Ellen, I see I needn't worry about you. You know where to turn when you need help."

"You taught me that, Megan, and I'm grateful."

"You called me mother when you prayed---I've always understood your feelings about that, but I loved hearing it."

"That's the one thing I don't think you have understood. You couldn't know how special your name is to me---what it's always meant! It was you who cared, you always let me know you were thinking about me---I knew it was you who loved me, not the woman I called mother!"

A rush of pain caught Megan. She moaned and I could see she was being carried farther away from me. I pushed her signal light. Her eyes opened to look at me with a light of love and sadness that tore my heart!

"Mother---I love you---mother---" The light in her eyes was gone. I felt someone's hand on my shoulder.

"Come, now, she can't hear you, it's too late." the nurse wore a mask of cool detachment as she steered me from the bed.

But a slight tightening of Megan's fingers around my own as I'd spoke had told me it had not been too late---she had heard! I looked up to find Doctor Fredon beside me. "Megan heard me, I know she did---it wasn't too late, it was just the right moment---"

I could see he thought I was about to become hysterical, and I thought perhaps I was, too! But what difference could it make now---I had been brave for Megan---

"You are right, Ellen, she heard you. As eager as Megan was to escape her pain, she was too stubborn to let go without hearing you say that. Isn't there someone I can call to be with you? Surely you aren't alone here?"

"No---I can manage---" I ran away from the room and

the faces and took the elevator down to the lobby. I fumbled for change to call a cab, then went outside in the fresh air to wait.

I looked up at the blue sky dotted with snowball clouds. Just a short hour ago I had been up there, hurrying to get to Megan. Now she was gone, now I could count on only myself---but that wasn't true, Megan had reminded me just a few moments ago---there was God. I could count on Him as surely as had Megan. I knew, and so did heaven, that this time I had truly seen a Christian die!

Megan's house seemed to be waiting for the moment she would return. I walked through each room, expecting at every turn to be overcome with grief and loss. Instead I found comfort in being among Megan's possessions.

Then I thought of father---we had not mentioned him! But there had been no room for him, there was only Megan and me, and, in that last moment---God. I was certain God had been there for Megan.

But Megan had known when she was with me for John's funeral that she was dying, and while she didn't tell me, in the end she had wanted me with her---she had to have known I might not arrive in time. Had she left a message for me before she went to the hospital? I was sure she had, and it would be here in her bedroom where she knew only, I would be!

I opened her desk and there it was, a cream-colored envelope with my name on it---I stood spellbound---I wanted to read it, but after I had---that would be all, Megan would slip beyond my reach! But my fingers had drawn the letter out and my eyes were eagerly seeking the words---

"To my dear daughter, Ellen---you know now the last secret I kept from you. I'm confident of your understanding as to why I chose to keep it. I want only for you to be happy, so please, live your life from now on with your own best interest at heart.

I have made all necessary arrangements; I could not bear to leave those decisions for you. Everything I have is yours, but Ellen, don't feel I would expect you to carry on as I have---sell the shops or keep them---they are yours, do with them as you wish.

My dearest Ellen, I left a gift for you at the cottage. When you see it you will know what I want most for you, for as most mothers I could not resist giving you one more bit of unasked-for advice! I know you will understand the love with which it is offered, whether or not you decide to heed it!

As for myself, Ellen, you made me so happy these past years, had I lived a century not one of those years would have been better, thank you, my little girl. I am almost tempted to sign this letter as "mother", but for you, I sign it instead as---Megan."

So she had understood why I hadn't called her mother, she had always understood! But who would understand me now---no one, No one would as Megan had! My grief could no longer be held at bay and I cried---for the long-ago little girl of Fox Hollow, and for the lonely girl I was today---right now I could not tell them apart---and for the first time, Megan could not help me.

Eleven

For the next two weeks I met with Megan's attorney and saw that things were again running smoothly at Paige's. There were a few calls from father, he always sounded oddly embarrassed as if he remembered all the years he hadn't called. There was a hollowness in his voice, and I could tell Megan's death had greatly affected him.

I had yet to visit the cottage. I hadn't been able to face it. I kept busy, forcing myself to crowd as much work as possible into each day---hoping I could sleep through the nights. But I would go tomorrow.

It dawned into a golden day, the late summer's sky was a bright, brittle blue and the ocean was just the way Megan loved to paint it.

I started up the steps. This comfortable cottage had always been Megan's favorite place. When I lived with her, we'd shared happy times here. Megan had set up her easel on the deck and worked for hours. She had a love for the ocean that transferred onto canvas with unfailing certainty. But she'd always been amazed when a customer would show interest in buying the seascapes I hung in Paige's, claiming they were not worth paying money to own.

I took a deep breath and opened the door. The moment I was inside I saw the gift Megan had mentioned in her letter. She had taken down *"Storm In September"*, a painting that had always made me uncomfortable. In It, Megan had departed from the soothing, almost sensuous scenes I'd known her to create and had thrown the ocean onto her canvas as a green frenzy, flinging itself in deep, boiling waves against an immovable barrier of jagged rock. Once, long ago, I'd taken it down to look at the date on the back. Megan had painted it the year I was born. At that time I had not suspected the significance of the painting's mood, but today I understood the frustration behind it.

Now in its place hung a landscape of Fox Hollow. I knew it was the only painting Megan had ever done that had nothing to do with the ocean. Then I noticed the small figure, in under the cedar trees---it was me---so this was Megan's advice! She thought I belonged at Fox Hollow! Megan couldn't have that without Mitch, Fox Hollow would be as lonely for me as this cottage had become.

I went out on the deck, facing the stiff breeze from the ocean. My eyes stung from the wind---or was it the tears--- it's so beautiful here---why can't I forget Fox Hollow---and Mitch!

The pier running out from the beach held the usual number of weekend fishermen, all looking so caught up in their efforts that I wished I also had nothing more pressing on my mind than which bait to use. Someone walking on the pier waved---at me, I guessed. I waved back, then went down the steps and walked the other way. I was sure it was one of the near-by cottage owners and I was in no mood for conversation or more condolences.

Walking faster, I tried to find solace in watching the sandpipers and seagulls and the constant roll and break of the waves.

On a dried piece of driftwood I sat down, staring out across the water---hearing voices in the wind---

"Ellen---" It came faintly, but when I heard it again I

looked back. It was Mitch!

I barely kept myself from running to him---*remember the other times you threw caution to the winds*---instead I stood, waiting, trying to hold back the towering feelings threatening to overwhelm me! Oh, the need to be held close in the arms of the one I loved---*but do you know Mitch loves you?* I didn't know---and I trembled as I spoke instead words that would hold him at a distance. "Hello, Mitch, this is certainly a surprise."

"No, my love---no words---they never seem to get us anywhere. Just come to me---"

If the waters rolled about our feet and the gulls continued wheeling overhead, I didn't know it---my heart flew above it all as I was crushed in his arms, lost in a haven I'd longed for and thought would never be mine!

He was still holding me close as he spoke. "I've nearly gone crazy waiting to see you!"

I drew back to look at him. "You've been here, waiting?"

"Thomas has talked so much about Megan and you---your lives here---I knew when you could come to the cottage you would be ready to make decisions. I took some vacation time and I've become very familiar with Onslow Bay---and that pier. I've done a lot of fishing to kill time and I don't even care for fish, fortunately I had no luck at all---until today!"

"Does father know you're here?" I wasn't sure why that mattered, but it did.

"He knows, but I'm here to speak strictly for myself, as I should have done before---come back with me!"

"I don't know where things stand anymore, so much has changed, and happened---everything is different!"

"That's right, Ellen, things are different---I know you need some answers, you'll find them---then you can decide if you'll be happy at Fox Hollow. I'll be there with you, you'll be safe!"

I stepped out of his embrace. A bit of the old caution I'd abandoned was returning. But Megan had done all she could to steer me back to Fox Hollow, and her advice to me had always been right---

"Sam will think I've forgotten her, and I want to give father something of Megan's---" I couldn't read everything in Mitch's face, but I saw the uncertainty change into hope, and the warmth in his eyes deepened---it was almost enough to convince me I was doing the right thing---almost.

We didn't fly back to Indiana on a commercial airline, returning instead with the same friend who had flown Mitch down. I had made all necessary arrangements with Megan's capable store manager, so I had no worries about business affairs in Wilmington.

Once again, I was at the Monroe County airport. Mitch was watching me closely, I could tell, as if he expected some reaction from me. I had been silent during most of the flight, wrapped in my thoughts, insulating myself against the time just ahead when I would face my father's grief---and against the time when I would have to tell him what Bertha and Rex intended to so with Fox Hollow if he played into their hands.

Now Mitch's jeep was approaching the west edge of town. "Would you mind taking me straight to the shop, my car is there and I'm really anxious to see Rachel."

"Sure thing. Are you feeling all right? You've been so quiet." He reached for my hand and held it tightly. His caring touch smoothed my aching hurt and I wanted nothing more at that moment than to forget the past and the future---to just stay beside him, close and safe, until I felt up to facing what was ahead.

And what was ahead? I wasn't certain---but I had a familiar, nightmare feeling, deep within---

Mitch took his hand away and turned the sharp corner into the alley behind the shop. "We made good time; Rachel hasn't closed yet." He shut off the engine and turned to face me.

"Thank you, Mitch, I'll drive on home after I've talked to Rachel."

"Ellen, don't stay on after closing to catch up on the bookwork---go home and get some rest." I had to smile at his stern tone of voice. "There. That's what I wanted to see--

-that smile!" He got out of the jeep and walked me to the back door of the shop.

"Have you noticed there is no moonlight---we are standing in an alley, in broad daylight?"

"Yes---I'm aware of all that---why?"

He wrapped his arms around me and kissed me deeply. My arms were clinging and my pulse was pounding before I made myself pull away.

"You see, Ellen---it's the same with or without moonlight! I'll call you later, just to say good night."

I went in the shop and found Rachel preparing to close. "Ellen! Couldn't call and let me know you were coming---it's so good to see you!" She hugged me enthusiastically. "Business has been great and I've been so anxious for you to get back and see for yourself.!"

"Rachel, you've been a godsend for me---I could never have managed without you! I'll help lock up and we can talk."

"Fine, but let's go to my place, I'd love a cup of something hot."

I followed Rachel's little car and parked mine beside it in front of her apartment. In her tiny kitchen she was soon pouring a fragrant tea into china cups. "You drink too much coffee, Ellen. You could still get hair on your chest---isn't that what Bertha used to tell you would happen when you were small and wanted coffee?"

I laughed, "Yes! I'd forgotten! This tea is delicious, but I want to get right to the point---since it's very likely I'll be staying here, Rachel, what would you think of going to Wilmington and being assistant manager for Paige's?" Our manager there is a lovely lady, you'd like her, but she'll be retiring in a year or so. She's been with Megan since I can remember---I'd love to know you were there to take her place."

"Ellen, I don't have to think about it---yes! ---I'd love to get away, and I want to continue working with you---this would be perfect for me!"

"I was hoping you'd think so! Megan has a lovely home in town, you can live there---it's beautifully furnished and I want to keep her things---I wouldn't have to worry with you there---and you can use the cottage on weekends---"

"And you can fly down for a vacation or just a weekend!" We laughed at each other. "Ellen, maybe I'd better not get carried away until we know for certain you're staying."

"Maybe, but it's fairly sure, I'll let you know something positive as soon as I do! I'm relieved to know you're interested---and I'm just realizing how tired I am! I'm going to Fox Hollow and get Sam, then home to bed! See you in the morning."

"O.K. Say, Ellen---we've had several days with hard rains, watch the road along Fish Creek---you know how it always gets during a rainy spell!"

The sun had already set. I'd spent more time talking and drinking tea with Rachel than I'd thought.

Soon I was well out into the countryside. The road climbed, then dipped into valleys. Deep ravines fell back from the road here, but soon it would run dangerously close to the creek. When my car lights caught it I saw the creek was full to overflowing---one would have to be careless for only a second to be in serious trouble. And on up ahead were the hairpin curves where John had died---I shivered. I just wanted to get Sam and myself safely back to town.

I tried not to look at the old church, abandoned now, or the Flagg's empty house, knowing how haunted they would appear in the deepening darkness. I was suddenly feeling again that sensation of something from a dream about to become reality. It made me eager for the lights of Fox Hollow.

As I drove through the cedars and started down the hill a stab of lightening stuttered across the night sky. Please---don't let it rain!

I parked at the house and ran up onto the porch. I knocked and waited, then knocked again. It was strange Bertha didn't answer. I went in, there was no one in sight so I went directly to father's study. The door was ajar, and I walked in.

"Hello---no one answered the door so I came on in."

Father looked up from his desk where numerous ledgers were scattered. "Well. You're back. Been expecting you any day. You should have called before you drove out---what if I hadn't been here?"

"I really just came for Sam. I knew either you or Ersey would be here. I thought we'd talk tomorrow---I'm not up to much more today."

"You do look tired---sit down. I'd have Bertha make coffee but she's off somewhere, haven't seen much of her today." He ran his hand through his hair as he spoke and leaned back in his chair.

He looked much as I'd expected, but there was something in his eyes that betrayed the calm exterior he posed behind---and lines I hadn't seen before were etched deeply along his mouth. I sat down reluctantly---and yet I didn't really want to leave---something told me to stay---that he wanted me to. Only a short time ago that would not have moved me---tonight it did.

I opened my purse and drew out the tissue-wrapped object I'd carried from Megan's house in Wilmington.

"I brought you something of Megan's. I'd never seen it until last week. I found it in her desk---in her bedroom."

He cupped his hands to receive it as if he didn't want to risk dropping it. I watched with a hard lump in my throat as he carefully pushed the tissue aside. He sat the tiny, gold fox on his desk. With his second attempt he managed to ask, "Are you sure you want to give this to me?"

"Yes. I think Megan would want you to have it."

"When I gave this to her, I told her she should always have golden things and soft furs to wear---she said she wanted no animal killed to keep her warm---and no man who'd do the killing! But I'm glad she kept the golden fox. You know, Megan could make me so angry in the very same moment I---she was the only woman who ever stood up to me---you're a lot like her---you've got her eyes, those hazel eyes---sometimes I see a look there and I---" despite his effort, a tear slid down his face.

It shattered my composure completely and I stood up. "Let's talk tomorrow---we're both tired. But there is something important I have to tell you, it's about Fox Hollow---"

"After tomorrow no one will need to worry about Fox Hollow, it will all be settled. I'll want to see you in the morning, you and Mitch."

"Mitch? Why?"

"Because I trust him---and I still think you two should get together---he's the only good idea I've ever had where you're concerned!"

I started to snap as angry retort, then stopped. He was grinning at me and I had to grin, too---we had both regained our balance. "Where is Sam?"

"Ersey put her in one of the kennels, I'm sure she'll be easy to find as he refused to put her in with my hounds."

Good for Ersey, I thought, as I went out to the car. I'd just drive down, get Sam and leave before anyone knew I was around. I passed the stables and stopped as close to the first kennel as I could and got out. Why wasn't the security light on---here away from the house it was totally dark. My eerie feeling had returned as soon as I'd left the house and now I wished Ersey was about.

There was an excited chorus of eager yapping as I neared the kennel fence. Sam wouldn't be here, father had said Ersey was keeping her apart---I turned toward the far kennel, walking with caution. Even so I bumped into the wire gate, it was standing open and blended so well with the darkness that I hadn't seen it in time.

Rubbing my skinned ankle, I looked around. Obviously, Sam was not here---would Ersey have put her in the stables---again lightening snapped on and off across the sky. I reassured myself that if it was going to rain at all it wouldn't be for a while yet---but it brought me out of my indecision and I hurried as fast as I dared toward the stables.

At the end of the double row of stalls was a small office. In it the light was on, surly Ersey would be there, and, I hoped, Sam!

The horses paid no heed as I passed, making my way easily in the darkened building. When I was near the office window that looked out into the stall area, I could see Ersey standing with his back to me.

The rush of relief I felt was checked as the outside door of the office flew open and Bertha burst in. I stayed where I was, hoping she would leave quickly so I could talk to Ersey. I couldn't handle hearing her babble on about how much Megan had meant to her, the only way I could avoid that was to stay hidden and wait.

"You seen Rex yet?" Bertha's voice carried easily. "I been expectin' him anytime, called him quite a while ago."

"No use in him comin'---you ain't doin' no business with Rex Post! I told you after I found out he sold Fox Hollow horses to those butchers that I ain't havin' him on the place!"

"Now you listen here---I got a chance to be more than hired help around here and I ain't givin' that up! In a couple months Thomas is gonna be fifty and that clause I had the brains to put in that deed is---"

"Forget that clause, Bertha, Thomas is gonna put Ellen back in his will, you know it well as me, and Rex sure ain't gonna help you with your crazy ideas!"

"Crazy!" It hissed from Bertha's clenched teeth. "We'll see who's crazy when I get back my land you and your shiftless ways lost---I ain't missin' out on this chance---it's the only one I got! I'm tired of havin' nothin' and this will make me rich---richer than Thomas Jordane hisself! You sure ain't never gave me nothin'---not even a family to raise!"

There was silence as they faced each other, Ersey pale and Bertha flushed and hot, sweat shining on her face. I didn't want to listen to their argument and now I knew Sam was not in the office. Bertha had been too afraid of the big dog the night she drove into town to see me and Megan to stay in a room with Sam.

A stir of fresh air moved over me, and I jerked around in time to see the stable door easing shut. Someone was walking toward the office. A horse stomped and bumped against its stall. I took advantage of the noise to move back into the shadows. I could see nothing. My eyes had been fastened to the bright window which made the stables much darker in contrast. I tried to quiet my breathing and shrank flatter against the smooth boards of the end stall behind me. Who was in here---could they see me? No, they would be watching the window as I had done---if only father would come to the stables---

Ersey moved and grabbed Bertha's shoulders. He was shaking her roughly. "Bertha---you're talkin' crazy again---" The strange couple framed by the window suddenly looked like a Punch and Judy puppet show and I held back a nervous urge to giggle.

The laughter that crackled from Bertha's body as she easily broke Ersey's hold on her sent a shock along my raw nerves.

"Too late, Ersey---too late for you to worry over what I'm doin'! I saw Ellen's car up at the house, she'll be down here for that dog of hers---where is it?"

"In that far kennel. I remembered that gate latch is loose and I came in here for some tools, I'm goin' to fix it now and then I'm goin' to stop whatever foolishness you're cookin' up!"

"Now you wait and listen to me, Ersey! I've got a plan for Ellen and it'll work same as everything else I've done---it was me that killed Nolan---I made sure he went down those stairs good and hard! Then I told it was Ellen that didn't watch him and everybody believed me---even you! Then Claudette started her whiskey nippin' and things worked out fine---Ellen's the last thing in my way---you just stay out of this---now that you know you've got to go along 'cause you ain't got the guts to do nothin' else!"

I huddled in my corner, feeling sick---I had heard Bertha admit what Megan and I suspected---and so had someone else---who?

Then in a rush of dark motion I saw the outline of a man block the window as he jerked the office door open. Bertha and Ersey swung to face him. It was Rex. Bertha was smiling triumphantly at him, her eyes bead-bright with a look that struck me as madness. Ersey slumped into a chair as if he'd had the breath knocked from his body, his putty-grey face looking ready to crumble.

Now---now was my chance---I could get help! I

dashed across the building to the side door. It stuck and I pushed against it with all my might---the rains had caused it to swell with moisture and it stubbornly resisted my frantic assault! Then, as I threw a desperate glance behind me, the door suddenly opened and I half fell outside, taking with me a quick impression of three surprised people as lights were switched on inside the stables.

Outside the security lights were at once turned on, exposing me with their blue-white stare. I moved quickly into deeper shadows. I was on the side of the stables farthest from the house and my car was well to my left, down by the kennels. Now I knew Sam had jumped against the gate and pulled the already loose latch out of the post, she was free, perhaps nearby---I'd have to worry about her later---now I had to hide myself.

I stood in the shadows, unable to decide what to do---Bertha and Rex were looking for me, I knew. But Ersey would help, he'd get father---wouldn't he? The wind pushed strongly at me, it was rising, carrying the scent of rain soon to come. I had to move.

Just as I was about to start toward my car, a form I couldn't recognize separated from the shadows, then merged again. My mouth went dry and I stared at the shapes around me, trying to distinguish between them. Sounds filled my ears---treefrogs and crickets joined the gusting wind as it fluttered leaves and scraped branches together. I wanted to scream at everything to stop so I could hear the footsteps I sensed were approaching!

Silently the form again separated itself from the dark and moved in my direction---I stood frozen for a moment longer, then found my voice and screamed for Sam so loudly my throat seemed to tear inside---then I could only run!

My feet seemed to regain a memory of their own as I flew across the wide expanse of grass between the kennels out toward the dark pastures! Automatically I dodged tree limbs and ducked through wooden fences, following childhood paths recalled just in time to direct my flight!

As I reached the edge of the woods it seemed to reach out and draw me in, as if it recognized me. I stood gasping, wondering if I was safe---but my heart was thudding so I couldn't tell if there were sounds of pursuit. I waited, crouched in thick undergrowth just inside the woods. My breathing eased and my senses grew sharper. I heard someone. From inside the darker woods looking out into the meadow I could see a man, half-running almost directly toward me. I huddled down and waited. He was at the edge of the woods, cursing under his breath---" always was wild as a damn fox!"

The wind took the muttered, out-of-breath words before I could be certain, but it had to be Rex---it could be no one else. I waited as he angled away, then straightened and started to move when I caught a movement out of the corner of my eye. Pushing back the impulse to plunge on, I waited. Someone else had been waiting too, but he had moved first and as he passed near me the moon broke through the clouds just long enough to show clearly who it was---Rex! Then who---no matter---I was going to have to save myself from two men probably as familiar with these woods as I was myself! That cold knowledge drove everything else out of my mind.

It seemed I had stood statue-still for ages, my body ached from the effort. I had to do something while I was reasonably sure of their location. I was afraid to risk crossing the open pasture a second time, my legs were trembling and now I would not have the element of surprise on my side---they were looking for me!

Staying along the woods' edge where the footing was quieter, I took the opposite direction an headed toward the footbridge. I was sure I was expected to try to reach the house and father, but if I could cross the bridge without being seen I'd go up the hill to the road---then I'd walk to the nearest house---help was not that far away!

Apparently, Rex and whoever was with him had no flashlights, perhaps I had arrived before Bertha had time to organize the plan she had expected to carry out. Now I could hear the creek running fast over the rocks. From the last bit of protection I'd have until I was across the bridge, I tried to make sure no one was hiding, waiting for me to try to cross.

I could see no one, the clouds had thickened until there was no moonlight---I had to try!

The wind whipped a thin, long briar in front of my face. I dodged, but it caught on the silk scarf about my neck and I jerked at it, entangling the scarf even more. As I undid the knot and let the scarf slip from my neck, I felt the first large drops of rain---they spurred me on and as I stepped onto the bridge it occurred to me that the nearly flooding waters could have weakened the old structure. I was nearly across when I found I'd been holding my breath with each step as if it would lighten the load, I almost laughed with giddy relief---I was across---

The vibrations told me as quickly as the pounding tread that I was caught---I turned, too weak-kneed to run--- the dark shape hurled itself at me and I tumbled to the board floor---"Sam!" I was crying with relief as she whined and licked my face. I tried to calm her and hold her still, the floor of the bridge was only five feet wide and there was a narrow board every now and then that supported the handrail, leaving wide gaps in between. I had no desire to find myself in the deep water below amid all the debris. I had to get Sam and myself off the bridge, if she had been heard as she crashed about through the woods she could easily lead Rex right to me!

I hurried Sam along and she was satisfied to trot close to my side. We had gone a few feet up the hill when I heard it, at first it seemed to be the wind---but then I heard the voice---words---

"Ellen---are you there---" I tried to shrink farther into the brush. I held Sam's collar and stroked her muzzle. She seemed to sense the need for quiet; she stayed still, ears cocked toward Rex's voice.

What did Rex think---that if he talked Sam would bark or somehow give our location away? He couldn't expect me to answer! I assumed he was joined by his friend, for I heard snatches---" I'll check---watch for her here---" I clamped my teeth tightly to stop their nervous chattering as Rex passed a few yards to my left. He was going to the Flagg house, I was sure. And on the other side of the creek someone was waiting for me---as soon as I could no longer hear Rex making his way up the hill, I urged Sam on again, heading straight across the hill to my right.

The undergrowth thinned and we were on quieter, moss covered ground. Then I realized where we were. There was once a fox den near here---old Brandy's---we scrambled uphill among taller trees, then came out onto a ledge protected above by an overhang of rock and scrubby growth---old Brandy's den!

I moved back into the hollowed-out area as far as I could bring myself to go. Sam settled herself between me and the opening. The rock ledge jutting out overhead served as an awning. I stared out into the wet, very black night as thunder rumbled about, Sam moved closer and I huddled beside her for warmth.

I closed my eyes and saw Bertha's smiling face and heard her wild laughter---I jerked up, cracking my head on the rock ledge above! I had actually drifted off to sleep for a moment---but now I could hear nothing but a deluge of rain. Somehow it made me feel safer. My aching head and limbs longed for sleep---Sam was calm---we were safe in old Brandy's den. I put my head on my arms and felt a tear slide down my face---but I was too exhausted to cry---

Thank you, God, for letting me know about old Brandy---and for helping me remember her tonight--- before my prayer was ended, I was asleep.

I woke to see Sam sitting patiently outside the den's opening. Carefully I sat up and felt my head---there was a slight bump, and my hands and arms were terribly scratched---but it was morning, and I was alive---I felt a fierce surge of elation!

"Sam, we fooled them---I wasn't called Foxey Locksey for nothing!" She came, wiggling and whining, and I rubbed her ears.

I peered out cautiously. The rain had stopped without my knowing, there was fog down below nearer the creek, and the sound of rushing water came muffled through it. I crawled out of the den and stood up gingerly---aches and pains jabbed at every move, but I was all right, and rather proud of myself as well!

I was trusting Sam to let me know if anyone was around, and we started off toward the bridge. I was sure Bertha and Rex would expect me to keep going in the opposite direction, so Fox Hollow would be the safest place. And I would go while there was still some morning fog to hide me, for already I could see the sun would burn its way through before too long. In the light the way to the footbridge seemed remarkably short. More debris had piled up among the rocks, crowding against the banks and catching on exposed tree roots.

Sam bounded on across the bridge ahead of me, intent on some real or imagined scent. I let her go, I did not really think there was any further danger---Bertha was no doubt in the hands of the police by now.

I looked down, the water swirled in large eddies directly under the floor of the bridge. I stepped off, relieved to be across.

"I been lookin' for you to come along!" Bertha stepped out onto the path directly in front of me, holding the scarf I'd lost last night. I could only stare, in no way prepared for the shock of seeing her!

"You seen yourself? You look like you slept in the woods!" She chuckled deeply, her face broadening widely like a spreading viper's. I pulled my eyes away, trying to think against the panic pushing into my mind. "Didn't sleep last night myself, wonderin' where you was and who you might be talkin' to!" Lightening quick, she grabbed my arm.

"Let go, Bertha, or I'll call my dog!"

"I didn't see no dog with you---Ersey let it get away last night before he got that lock fixed---but you know that--- you were in the stables listenin' when you had no business bein' there!"

"It was my business---" I stopped. I didn't dare add fuel to the fire in her eyes. "Where's Ersey---and father?"

"Lookin' for help, are you? Won't do no good. Ersey ain't feelin' good and Thomas is back at the house, I think he's about ready to start lookin' for you at the bottom of this creek---which is just where he's gonna find you! They looked these woods over all night---but I knew you'd find a hidin' place, you was in these woods all the time when you was a kid---so I snuck down to wait for you to start to the house---I had you figured!" She increased the pressure on my arm, forcing me backward toward the foot-bridge.

"Sam!" I shouted. "Here, Sam!"

"Told you I know you ain't got that dog here---now shut---" the noise in the brush stopped her. Sam trotted out and came toward us, her tongue lolling wetly out of her mouth. "It's gonna attack---stop it!" Bertha's voice was shrill.

Sam stopped, as if to size up the situation, then advanced with a slow, measured step. Bertha kept her hold on my arm and moved behind me, awkwardly pulling me with her onto the bridge.

Bertha's eyes were riveted on Sam. When Ersey came down the path I was weak with relief, "Ersey---do something---" but he came on in the same slow, almost staggering shuffle, as if what he saw was of no real concern. He was as grey-faced as he'd looked last night in the stables, his eyes were red and he was still in the clothes he'd worn then.

"I tried to warn you, Ellen, I called you when you came back and told you to stay with Megan---you didn't listen, so I put that note in the shop---knew if you was here you'd stir this all up again---tried to keep this from happenin'---"

"Ersey! Shut up and call that dog off---it's a killer---" Bertha was trying to keep me between herself and Sam, who was posing no threat but merely sniffing around trying to find what had Bertha as excited. Berth's movements were making the bridge sway more than usual and with the rush of water scrambling past I felt a wave of dizziness.

"Ersey, call Sam---this bridge isn't safe, we've got to get off!" But Ersey seemed unaware of everything except Bertha and he stumbled onto the bridge, still talking, his eyes pinned on Bertha. I doubted if he was truly aware I was there.

A slight tremor passed through the bridge---or was it

just Ersey's additional weight. But as if she sensed danger, Sam turned and trotted to the bank, then paced back and forth, first barking then yapping, adding to the alarm.

Now Ersey was directly in front of us. "I tried to fix things for you, Bertha, I've told Thomas what you done, and I tried to tell him why---it ain't really your fault---I'm sorry I lost your homeplace---I did what I could but I never could suit you---then you killed that baby boy---makes me wild to know you done such a thing---"

Bertha's hold on me had eased when Sam left the bridge, now she had only the fabric on my light jacket clenched in her hand. I tried easing away but she held me just as firmly, even though she was staring unblinkingly at Ersey, seemingly hypnotized by his voice.

I realized Sam was no longer barking and I tried to look around Ersey to see where she had gone. I barely managed to choke back a sob of hysterical relief when I saw Mitch and father coming toward the bridge, Sam walking calmly beside them. But Mitch was motioning frantically for me to stay quiet and I forced myself to obey. At father's questioning look I slowly brought my left hand up to point at Bertha's unshakable grip on my sleeve.

I caught my breath sharply. The bridge moved---it was subtle, but unnatural. I saw that neither Bertha nor Ersey were aware of it. We had to get off---

"May as well let Ellen go, Bertha, ain't no reason to keep on with this." Ersey's words surprised me and I looked at Bertha who was now standing beside me facing Ersey..

"You told Thomas what I done?" It seemed to be all she had heard. Again I tried to ease my jacket sleeve from her grip.

A wave from father caught my attention and he had to repeat his signal before I understood what he wanted me to do. Slowly with my left hand I unbuttoned my jacket. Ersey was talking to Bertha, still holding her attention or it would not have worked, but I had shrugged my left arm out of its sleeve when the bridge shivered again against the onslaught of rising, muddy water. This time we were all put off balance and as Bertha bumped forward into Ersey I stepped backward, drawing my right arm free. One step, then another and I was past Ersey who still seemed oblivious to all except his wife---now I was moving as fast as the angle of the bridge would allow toward Mitch's outstretched hand---I was nearly there---the bridge swung left, then right and I felt the ground I'd just touched crumbling beneath my feet as the anchoring pulled out of the soft earth---

I was in cold water up to my waist, kept from being swept into the rapid current by Mitch's strong hands. He pulled me against the spongy bank, up and out of the swirling water. Then I was on solid ground, wrapped in Mitch's arms and unable to believe it!

"Put this on---" Mitch took off his jacket and I hurried into it, but I was shaking now, too much to work the zipper. "I'll do that. Wait here---" his eyes traced my face, then he turned and went to help father.

I got up, unsteady and shiveringly cold, and followed.

Ersey was lying on the ground, unmoving. "He's dead. It's my guess his heart gave out, he'd been having some trouble but didn't want anyone to know---wouldn't see a doctor---" Father stood up and put his arm about my waist, turning me away. "We'd better get you to the house and get some help."

"Bertha---what happened to her---"

"She was swept into those eddies---never made a sound---it'll take some while to find her---"

I turned away, sickened. Sam rubbed against my legs and I bent down to pat her. She poked her long nose in my face and licked at the mud caked on my cheek.

"Ellen, "Mitch drew me up close beside him, "Let's go, you need coffee and a hot bath."

"Can you tell us now where you were all night?" Father was just behind us as the path would not allow us to walk three abreast. "I know you're tired, but we've been so damned worried!"

As I told how Sam and I spent the night I stopped shivering, walking warmed me as did Mitch's arm that held me close to him as we came out of the trees into the early sunshine.

"Should have known you'd be all right." father's voice was gruff, "but it's been one hell of a night for all of us! I felt like a fool, finding out you were in trouble while I sat in my study!"

"How did you know?"

"Rex called me on the phone in the stables and said there was trouble, to get down there and he'd explain the rest later, but we had to find you first---I didn't know then what you were running from!"

"But Rex was---"

"You were running from Rex?" Mitch asked.

"Yes---and another man I didn't recognize---it was too dark."

"Ellen, that was me! I called you at the Birkdale's house as I told you I would, but you weren't there, I called Rachel and she said you'd come out here to get Sam. You should have been back by that time; I was worried and drove out. I got here just when Rex called your father!"

"I spent the night hiding---for nothing?"

"It sure kept you out of Bertha's reach---she didn't think Rex or Ersey would try to stop her and she didn't mean for you to live to tell what you'd heard---but Rex wanted no part of murder."

"Then Rex was actually trying to help me!"

Father spoke. "Rex had given up on Fox Hollow and was coming to tell Bertha that last night, that's why he was here and heard her admit to killing Nolan. Ellen, I don't know what to say to you---"

I shook my head. "We won't talk about all that now."

He continued. "Rex and Ersey came to me about an hour ago and told me everything. Seems Bertha just went crazy when they told her she'd have to admit to what she had done. When we couldn't find her, we knew she'd slipped out to look for you---Sam's commotion down by the bridge had a lot to do with our arriving in time."

We were at the kitchen door. "Poor old Ersey," Father muttered as he went in. I looked at Mitch. "He'll be all right, Ellen, here, get those wet shoes off, you don't need them now."

It was strange to walk into the kitchen and see father at the stove, making coffee.

"This will be ready by the time you shower, don't dawdle!" He was dialing the telephone as he spoke.

Mitch grinned at me as I went up the stairs. I went to the room that had once been mine, it was a guest room now, but as the hunt season was over there were only empty rooms. I stared at my reflection---wet, muddy and tired and strained---and I smelled of creek mud. I wondered what I'd put on, my clothing was ruined.

The fragrant soap and comforting hot water blocked my mind to everything else as I luxuriated in the everyday things that were now such pleasures. As I was toweling my hair father called through the door.

"Here's a robe, and slippers if they'll stay on your feet. Afraid I'm not your size. Coffee's ready."

And I could smell the rich aroma as I went down the hall, swathed in one of father's robes and shuffling to keep his slippers on. The stairs proved too much, and I gave up on the slippers. Mitch met me on the bottom step.

"At least I'm clean, so no remarks!"

His eyes suggested, even though he took my advice and said only, "But you look so fetching!"

"You two! Coffee's in the study, we'll eat later---Ellen, I want to tell you something before the police get here," he was pouring our coffee. I sat beside Mitch on the leather sofa, tucking my feet up under the robe. I sipped, and the warmth reached through me, relaxing me and acting as a buffer against the shock I could still feel waiting to move in.

"About Fox Hollow---I'm going to make some big changes---someone once told me this would be a perfect place for bridle trails and a wildlife refuge. I've had enough of the hunts, I certainly don't need the money, so I'm dissolving the Fox Hollow Hunt Association. What do you think about it, Ellen?"

My cup was rattling against my saucer and Mitch took it from me to place it on the coffee table. "I---I'm pleased--- more than I can say---and I'm proud you'd do this---I know who that someone was, and I know she's proud of you too!' I choked on the last words and turned to Mitch's arms, overcome by my tears. He held me gently, his lips warm against my forehead.

"Take care of her, Mitch." I heard father say as he left the room.

"That's what I want to do, Ellen," he made me look at him. "Do you love me?"

I put my arms around his neck and brought his head down next to mine. "Yes," I whispered close to his ear, "I love you!"

He met my lips, his arms coming about me hard and tight. I was shaking when we drew apart.

I smiled through new tears. "We'll have to try that again sometime when I'm not crying and see if it works as well! Or do you prefer your women with a wet face?"

"I'll love you just as much when you're bone-dry---if you'll try to learn to recognize me in the dark!"

I laughed, "It's a deal!"

An impatient bark from the hall brought Mitch to his feet. I'll let Sam in to keep you company while I give Thomas a hand with things. I won't be long---stay right here and rest---drink your coffee---but don't go anywhere---

"I'm not about to in this robe---fetching though it may be!"

He stood a moment more in the doorway looking at me as if he thought I might yet disappear, then closed the door softly.

Sam settled in front of the sofa, stretching out as if she planned to sleep the day away.

I refilled my cup and sipped the hot coffee. *It's really quite good---I wouldn't have thought father could brew a good pot.* I looked at his desk. Megan's gold fox was still there, where I was sure it would always be---a quick, tiny glitter flashed---had it winked? Or had it been the sunshine reaching through the windows to twinkle in its eye---I smiled---*Yes, Megan, I know---everything will be all right now!*

Made in the USA
Monee, IL
04 July 2021

72171022R00098